ARUBA

BAD BOYS ON THE BEACH BOOK THREE

KIMBERLY FOX

ARUBA
Bad Boys on the Beach
Book Three

By KIMBERLY FOX

Sign up to Kimberly Fox's exclusive newsletter to hear about new releases and to get exclusive content, including **a bonus chapter** from this book!

Sign up at:
www.AuthorKimberlyFox.com/newsletter.html

Do you like Paranormal Romance?
Kimberly Fox has an extensive paranormal romance catalog that she writes under Kim Fox.
Check out her PNR books at
www.AuthorKimFox.com

To the head lifeguard at my kid's pool.
Thanks for the hours of visual enjoyment this summer.

CHAPTER ONE

DAY ONE

Julia

"You! American girl! Out!" the bus driver shouts as he glares at me through the rear-view mirror.

I gulp as all of the locals on the bus turn and look at me with blank faces. "Okay," I squeak as I hop out of my seat and struggle to pull my huge bag down the narrow aisle.

A few of them snicker as the strap of my Louis Vuitton suitcase gets snagged on a seat.

"What happened to the tourist bus?" an older guy asks as he laughs at me. "They couldn't fit your enormous bag in it?"

"She wants to experience the true Aruba," another guy from the back calls out. "Complete with gum on the seats and broken air conditioning."

The people laugh and giggle as I finally get my strap unhooked and yank my oversized suitcase up to the driver.

"I thought you were taking me to the Alanda Resort," I

say, looking out the dirty windshield of the local bus. All I see is a dirt road and dense jungle around me.

He shakes his head impatiently. "Down there," he says, pointing to a wall of thick jungle bush. "Now out!"

"But, I thought—"

"Out!" he shouts, whipping his head back and glaring at me. I can see myself in his mirrored sunglasses. I look sweaty, stressed, tired—the opposite of what I should be feeling while on vacation.

"Okay, okay," I mumble to myself as I drag my suitcase down the steps. I turn and look at him through the open door once I'm outside. "Excuse me, where did you say it—"

He closes the door in my face before I can finish and drives off, covering me in a disgusting cloud of dust and exhaust fumes.

I already hate Aruba.

It's hot, sticky, and *way* out of my price range.

I sigh as I drag my heavy suitcase down the dirt road toward the spot where the bus driver had pointed, picturing my friends hanging around the pool with drinks in their hands and hot guys at their sides.

This is the third destination wedding I've been to in three years. Megan was the first when she married Lucas in Cancun, Tanya was next when she said her vows to Ethan in Belize, and now it's my best friend Cynthia's turn. She's marrying her hot Navy SEAL, Chase.

I'm the only single one left. Single with absolutely no prospects.

The closest thing I have to a prospect is Andy Hanson. He asked me to marry him a few weeks ago.

He's in my kindergarten class and only five years old, but the way I'm going, I'll be looking him up in thirteen years to see if the offer still stands.

I wipe my sweaty forehead as I turn down the dirt road that hopefully leads to the resort. I should have been in the air-conditioned luxury bus for rich tourists like everyone else in the wedding group, but all of my credit cards were maxed out along with my options.

It turns out that flying from Buffalo to Dallas, then from Dallas to Bogota, Columbia, waiting in the hot crowded airport for seven hours, and then flying from Bogota to Aruba on South America's oldest plane is three hundred dollars cheaper than the group rate that Cynthia and Chase offered us.

Last year, I wouldn't have thought twice about slapping down another credit card to pay for the extra luxury, but that was last year. Debtors weren't calling me every fifteen minutes last year, my credit cards worked last year, and I wasn't stuck living in my parent's basement because I was evicted from my apartment. Last year was awesome.

This year sucks.

I slap a mosquito the size of a hummingbird, crushing him on my arm as I walk up to the booth with the two security guards inside. They're watching an old episode of *Home Improvement* in Spanish. They look annoyed that I'm interrupting it.

"Yes?" the one standing up asks as he stares at me.

"I have a reservation here." I pull the booking paper out of my purse and offer it to him.

He just stands there with his hands on his hips, not taking the paper. "Where is your bus?"

"I took the local bus from the airport," I say, slapping another bug on my sweaty neck. "It was cheaper."

"The guests always come in on a bus."

I huff out a breath as I raise my arms and make a show of looking around me. "Well, I'm all out of buses."

I'm all out of buses, I'm all out of money, and I'm all out of giving any fucks. I'm hot, tired, annoyed, and if this guy doesn't lift up that goddamned bar soon, I'm going to go all Tim Allen on his ass.

The guy sitting down laughs at the TV and the one interrogating me turns to see what Jonathan Taylor Thomas shenanigans he missed.

Fuck this.

I duck under the yellow bar and curse under my breath as I charge up the road to the resort.

"Hey!" the security guard shouts as he runs out of the booth and follows me.

I just ignore him as he walks alongside me, squawking something into his radio.

"Yeah, call your friends," I say, gritting my teeth as I charge down the road. *You're going to fucking need them with the way I'm feeling right now.*

The path turns, and the gorgeous resort finally comes into view. I would stop to admire the intricately carved wooden walls, the high straw ceilings, and spectacular gardens with the huge tropical flowers if I wasn't about to get arrested any second now.

I arrive at the marble steps, and three more security guards come rushing out of the lobby. They stand in front of me like a sweaty wall, blocking my path to free drinks, beach, pool, shitty buffet food, and my best friend's wedding. They're going to need more than three security guards to stop me from getting to all of that.

An older Dutch man comes rushing out and smiles as he approaches me. He's wearing dress pants and a buttoned-up shirt over his tanned skin. "Can I help you, Miss?" he asks.

"Yes," I say, raising my chin in the air. "You can call off

these goons. I thought Alanda was a resort not a prison. What kind of welcome is this?"

"I'm sorry," he says, clasping his hands together and bowing his head. "Our guests always come in on a bus."

"I did come in on a bus," I snap back. I have the receipt of fifty cents to prove it. I hand him my reservation paper and he nods as he looks it over.

He says something to the security guards in a language I don't understand and they all walk away, looking disinterested. I turn back and give the original security guard a dirty look before he turns and hurries back to catch the end of *Home Improvement*.

"I see you're in the Taylor-Connor wedding group," he says, smiling at me. "The rest of the guests arrived before lunchtime."

Good for them. I was sitting in an airport in Colombia.

"Julia!" Megan calls out from the lobby. "She's over here, guys!"

I grin as Cynthia and Megan come rushing down the stairs in nothing but bikinis with sarongs wrapped around their waists. I meet them half way up the stairs, and they swallow my tired body in a hug.

"We've been waiting for you here all day," Cynthia says after kissing my temple.

I take the white slushy drink out of her hand and drink half of it in one gulp. "I got here as fast as I could," I say, grimacing as the brain freeze hits me.

"How was Colombia?" Megan asks with a chuckle.

"Hot. Crowded. A kid with chocolate on his fingers touched my Dolce & Gabbana dress." My jaw clenches just thinking about it. *I hate that kid.*

"I'll never understand how flying past Aruba and then

doubling back on another plane would be cheaper than flying direct," Cynthia says, shaking her head.

I sigh. "I don't know, but it is."

"We could have covered the difference for you," she whispers. "We really wouldn't have minded."

"I got here, didn't I?" I say, hoping she'll drop the subject. I may have negative seventy-six thousand dollars in credit card debt, but I'm not about to take charity from my best friend and her soon-to-be husband.

"Miss Cynthia," the Dutch man says, smiling as he walks over. "I'll check Miss Julia in immediately while you all catch up."

"Thank you, Lars," Cynthia says, smiling back at him. "He's the owner of the resort," she says when he's gone with my paper. "He's been great."

"Julia!" Tanya calls out as she waddles down the steps toward us. She's seven months pregnant and looking absolutely stunning. "Sorry, I had to go pee. For the thirty-sixth time since I got here."

I try to give her a hug, but my arms can barely reach her body with her huge stomach between us. "How did it go on the plane?" I ask. Tanya is terrified of flying.

"How do you think?" she asks with a shrug. "I had airsickness mixed with pregnancy sickness. I spent most of the flight crying in the bathroom."

Sounds like my flight, minus the puking.

"Well, we're all here now," I say, plastering a smile onto my sweaty face. I am the maid of honor on this trip, and it's my duty to make sure the party runs smoothly. "Let's get this wedding week started!"

The owner, Lars, comes back with the key cards to my room. He hands them to me and then takes my suitcase to have it brought up to my room. "I apologize for the way security acted," he says, bowing his head. "I upgraded you to a beachfront room."

"Is it going to cost extra?" I ask, holding my breath.

"Not a penny extra," he says, motioning us into the resort with his arm. "It's on me."

"Thank you, Lars," Cynthia says as we head inside.

"What happened with security?" Megan asks as we pass a gorgeous marble fountain. "Did they get a little too frisky when they patted you down?"

"No, I'm sweaty and gross," I say, swallowing hard when I see the pool in the distance. It looks so wet and cool and refreshing. "They wouldn't let me in, let alone touch me."

"I'm sorry, but I don't feel bad for you," Tanya says, looking me up and down with a sigh. "I would kill to be as sweaty and gross as you right now. I'm like that in an air-conditioned room. Out here, I have sweat pooled up in cracks I didn't even know I had."

"You look beautiful, Tanya," Cynthia says as she slides her arm over her shoulders. "You're having a baby. What can be more beautiful than that?"

Tanya lets out a sigh as she waddles beside us. "I don't know. Maybe a woman who doesn't let out half the water in the pool when she gets in."

"You shouldn't be complaining, Tanya," Megan says with a grin. "You always wanted bigger tits and now you have them. They're *huge*."

All four of us laugh as we look at Tanya's breasts. They have grown significantly since she's gotten pregnant. The clasp on her bikini top is hanging on for dear life.

"They hurt my back," she says, looking miserable. "I don't know how Sofia Vergara does it. If I had boobs like hers, my back would look like a question mark."

"I'll help you carry them," Megan says with a mischievous grin. "If you let me stick my face in there and motor-boat them."

Tanya laughs. Megan is always good at making her best friend laugh. "I didn't realize you liked big boobs so much."

Megan grins. "I like big boobs and I cannot lie," she raps like a nerdy Sir Mix-a-Lot. "You other bitches can't deny."

Tanya joins in for the next line:

"That when a preggers waddles by,

poking hard nipples in your eye,

with boobs that look as veiny as a map of Shanghai,

you get *sprung*."

"All right," I say, interrupting them with a wave of my hand. "Can I get some alcohol in me before you turn this wedding vacation into a no-talent talent show?"

Megan and Tanya both narrow their eyes on me. "Don't ever interrupt us mid-jam again," Megan warns.

"So not cool," Tanya says, shaking her head.

"How about you two go practice by the pool?" Cynthia says, pulling me away from them. "I'll walk Julia up to her room."

"Good idea," Megan says with an evil stare. "I wouldn't want to have to pop a cap up in here." They both start throwing up gang signs at me with their hands as they walk away.

I laugh. The only gang those two could join with their flowered bikinis and complete lack of street skills is The Get Along Gang.

Megan leans into Tanya as they turn around. "We're going to miss the show," she whispers. "I want to see her freak out." I'm not meant to hear that, but I do.

Cynthia is stiff and tense with an uncomfortable smile on her face. She heard them too.

"What is she talking about?" I ask, staring at my best

friend. "What am I going to freak out about?" I gasp. "Am I sharing a room with Tanya's Aunt Ophelia?"

I had brought a boyfriend to Tanya's wedding in Belize and Cynthia was forced to stay in a room with Tanya's perv of an aunt. She had porn playing on the TV the entire week and offered to share her extensive collection of dildos and vibrators. It's not like Cynthia to get even like this, but with my bad luck lately, I wouldn't count it out.

"Don't worry," she says, shaking her head. "Ophelia is not here. You heard Lars. You have a beautiful beachfront room all to yourself."

I stop walking and stare at her as I cross my arms over my chest. "Cynthia," I say, tapping my foot. I'm not in the mood to play games. "What is it?"

The bride laughs nervously as she taps her bottom lip with her finger, not wanting to tell me. "Maybe you should get a drink first."

"*Cynthia!*"

"Or six."

"Hey, look," she says, taking a breath of relief as she looks past me over my shoulder. "Chase! Ethan! Come say hi!"

I turn with my heart pounding and my jaw clenched as the two Taylor brothers come strutting over looking hotter than ever. They're both shirtless, wearing only bathing suits that hang down their muscular legs. Every female head in the lobby turns and follows them as they walk over.

They're both tall, muscular, inked up, gorgeous—and completely off limits. The older brother, Ethan, is married to Tanya, and the younger Navy SEAL brother, Chase, is about to be married to the question-dodging woman standing next to me.

"You made it!" Chase says, giving me a hug as he arrives.

Ethan smiles as he hugs me next, swallowing me in his hard muscles. "This place is amazing! Julia, you have to see the beach!"

"I will," I say, nodding as I shoot a sideways glance at Cynthia. "I'll just finish talking with Cynthia, and then I'll go see it."

"It's okay," Cynthia says, hopping over to join the boys. "We'll finish talking once you've showered and are feeling better. I'll see you at the beach."

I groan as I watch her hurry away, frantically waving for the Taylor brothers to join her.

"I guess we'll see you at the beach," Chase says with a shrug before walking backward to catch up to his fiancée.

"Hey Chase! Any hot Navy SEAL friends down there?" I ask hopefully.

"Oh, yeah," Chase says with a nod. "*Tons* of them."

I grin as I watch them walk to the pool. I've been bugging Chase to set me up with one of his hot Navy SEAL friends for months, and now I'll have my pick of them.

Maybe this vacation won't be so bad after all.

Still. I can't help but get a sinking feeling in my stomach, wondering what Cynthia is hiding from me.

My spirits start to lift as I walk through the stunning resort on the way to my room. The Caribbean sun is shining, there are smiles on everyone's faces, and the palm trees are swaying in the warm breeze.

When the beach comes into view, I feel better than ever. I've been so stressed out the last few months as I've been forced to face the tsunami of debt that I've stupidly accumulated over the past few years. I have a bit of a shopping addiction, and with only a kindergarten teacher's salary to pay it off, it added up fast. *Really* fast.

I step off the path, slip out of my Fendi sandals, and let my toes sink into the warm powdery white sand as I take a deep breath of the fresh salty breeze. The palm trees are dancing above my head as soft Caribbean music plays from a beach bar somewhere behind me. The ocean is a turquoise blue that can only be found on tiny islands deep in the Caribbean Sea.

"Mmmm," I moan as I close my eyes, letting the sun kiss my eyelids. I decide to let myself relax this week and not think about my crushing mountain of debt that's been weighing on my shoulders.

I glance down the beach and a beautiful sight catches my eye: Eight shirtless men playing a game of beach volleyball.

Good boy, Chase.

Those are his Navy SEAL friends. All muscular. All hot. All about to be fighting over who gets to make this the best week of my life.

I grin as I look around and see a dozen or two horny women watching them. *They're all mine ladies.*

This week is going to be amazing. I don't care what Cynthia has to tell me. It can't possibly ruin the week for me.

I take a deep breath, smile, and turn around, ready to have the best week of my life.

"Hey, Mosquito Bites," a voice calls out from behind me. A voice I haven't heard in years.

My stomach drops as cold chills run through my body despite the hot sun beating down on me.

No.

His deep masculine voice sounds like nails on a chalkboard.

Tucker.

I turn and see him walking toward me with an arrogant grin on his frustratingly handsome face.

This is what Cynthia didn't want to tell me about.

Her brother is here.

And I'm trapped on this resort with him for a week.

Kill me now.

CHAPTER TWO

DAY ONE

Julia

If I knew Tucker was here, I would have turned around and hopped on the first plane back to Colombia. And then I would have hijacked the plane and flown it straight into the ocean.

And no, I'm not being dramatic. You don't know Tucker.

"I've been waiting for you," he says, grinning as he struts forward. I cross my arms over my chest and keep my eyes off him. He's like the sun. Stare at him for too long and you'll get burned.

"Oh, that's a coincidence," I say, straining to keep my eyes off him. "Because I've been *waiting* for you. To drop dead."

"I'm sorry to disappoint," he says as he stops in front of me. I keep my eyes locked on a nearby palm tree.

"Well, that is your specialty," I say, holding my breath. "You've always been good at disappointing people."

"Are you still holding grudges from high school?" he

asks. I can hear the smirk in his voice. *Ugh*. Did I mention I hate this guy?

I pry my eyes off the palm tree and turn to him with a fierce glare. Finally looking at him takes me by surprise, and I have to concentrate on keeping my eyes narrowed on his face.

This is not the same Tucker I knew when I was sixteen. The misbehaving bad boy who liked to tease me and make me squirm has turned into a man. He's taller than I remember, and his large frame has filled out with thick muscle. Tattoos decorate his round arms—like he needs any decoration for them. They're beautiful on their own, but the intricately inked tattoos add a look of danger that suits Tucker perfectly.

His stomach is shredded with abs that are calling me to touch them. My fingertips tingle just thinking about it.

I squeeze my hand into an angry fist as I look him in his honey-colored eyes. "I'm not holding grudges. I just don't like you."

"Sounds like a grudge to me," he says with a laugh. "You should let it go. Holding grudges will give you premature wrinkles."

This guy is going to give me premature wrinkles. *And* gray hair. *And* a migraine.

I already feel one coming on.

"Why are you even here?" I ask with my hands planted on my hips.

"I'm the brother of the bride. Of course, I'd be here."

"I thought you had an important business deal that you couldn't get out of."

"I got out of it," he says with a shrug. "I'd never let Cynthia down like that."

I grit my teeth as I look up at him. He's got a gorgeous

face, I'll give him that, but it's still incredibly smackable. Every time I look at him, I think that he'd look much better with a red handprint on his cheek. A handprint in the exact same shape as mine.

"Are you here with a guy?" he asks, taking a quick look around.

My eyes fall to his strong jaw and soft lips. My heart starts beating faster when his lips part and I get a glimpse of his straight white teeth underneath. Tucker always had the nicest smile, but I always hated it. Whenever I saw him smiling, it was usually at my expense.

He turns back to me and my guilty eyes dart up to his. He smiles, and a flood of warmth fills my body.

I need a cold shower.

Oh, crap. I just realized how horrible I look right now. I've been in four airports in the past twelve hours and it shows. I have to get to my room and show Tucker what he missed out on.

"I came by myself," I say, raising my chin in the air, "but I'll be leaving with one of *those* guys."

I turn and look at the gorgeous men playing volleyball on the beach, trying to make Tucker jealous.

"Chase's Navy SEAL friends," I say with a nod. "Apparently they've been fighting over who gets to ask me out."

"Wow," he says, nodding as he looks over at them. "Sounds like you're doing great for yourself."

"I am," I lie. "I'm doing awesome."

"Awesome."

"What about you?" I ask after a moment of silence. "Cynthia said you have a new girlfriend. Is she here? I would love to meet the girl who can put up with you. She must have the resilience of Nelson Mandela."

"We broke up," he says with a grin.

"Ahh, that's too bad," I say, trying to hold in a laugh. "Did she finally get to know the real you and then claw her eyes out?"

"I broke up with her."

"Tucker, if you meet someone who can stand to be around you for more than four and a half minutes, you should hold onto them for life. There's so few people out there who can put themselves through that kind of torture."

He laughs. I have to look away because the sight is making my breath quicken.

Thank God.

Cynthia's mother is walking over holding an iPad over her face. She's talking to it as she nearly walks into a tree.

"Mom," Tucker says. "Put that thing down before you walk into the pool and drown."

She looks at us in shock. "You two are actually talking to each other? Without fighting? Without the police having to watch over you? I have to get a picture of this! Nobody is going to believe me."

She turns the iPad toward us. Tucker and I are visible on the screen. I look worse than I thought.

"Say hello to Facebook," she says, smiling. "This is going on my Facebook page."

"Everything goes on your Facebook page," Tucker says, placing his hand on the iPad and lowering it. "Why don't you put the iPad away and actually live your life in person?"

Cynthia's mom Amy is obsessed with social media. She lives life like an Instagram celebrity but with two main differences: she only has forty-six friends, and almost all of her pictures have her thumb blocking a part of the photo.

Amy rolls her eyes at her son as she turns off the iPad. "I finally see my son and he makes fun of me."

"I'd like to see you too," Tucker says with a laugh. "But

all I've seen is your body with a big white iPad covering your head. I think you're obsessed."

"No, I'm not," she says, looking offended. "Julia what do you think? Do I post too much on Facebook?"

My newsfeed is full of minion memes, inspirational quotes, and pictures of her thumb, all courtesy of her, but I'm not about to take Tucker's side. I would take Lucifer's side over his.

"I think your son should spend more time with his mother rather than criticizing her," I say, smirking at him.

"Thank you," she says, smacking Tucker's muscular arm. "See? Be nice to your mother. Let's take a selfie."

I sneak away as Amy grabs her son with one hand and holds up her iPad with the other. Tucker's eyes never leave my body as I hurry away to my room.

I can finally breathe easier once I turn into the building's stairwell, out of his view, but I'm still amped up. I quickly find my room, not even stopping to admire the stunning landscaping, the beautiful art on the walls, or the breath-taking view of the ocean along the way.

I'm on the top floor of the closest building to the beach. Room 1304.

"Wow," I gasp when I open the door and see the luxurious room with the turquoise water of the ocean visible through the sliding glass doors. *If my debt collectors could see me now.*

They'd probably have me arrested.

The room is so nice that I'm almost able to calm down from my meeting with Tucker. Almost.

My heart is still pounding angrily in my chest as I check out the sick bathroom with the walk-in shower and enormous tub. *I have to get one of these for my parent's basement.*

I grab my suitcase that's waiting for me by the door and

toss it on the king-sized bed. Horrible memories of Tucker come flooding back as I take out my clothes and hang them up in the closet.

I've been best friends with Cynthia since kindergarten when I got an expired milk carton at school and the cute girl with the wild brown curly hair took pity on me and shared half of hers. We've been inseparable ever since.

Cynthia is my favorite person in the world. Her only fault, which isn't really her fault, is that Tucker came attached to her.

Her older brother tormented and teased me all through elementary school and then just got worse once high school came around. He broke my toys, pulled my hair, and called me every name in the book. He even called me Voodoo*lia* for a month after he caught me with a voodoo doll that had a picture of his face taped to its head.

But his favorite mean name to call me was Mosquito Bites. He called me that after puberty hit and my breasts started growing. They grew for about a week and then stopped for a whole year, leaving me with the tiniest little buds that looked like mosquito bites.

I yank my empty suitcase off the bed and throw it into the closet as I huff over to the mirror in the bathroom and check out my breasts. *Well, they don't look like mosquito bites anymore.*

He's going to pay for calling me that.

I'm grinning maniacally as I get my hottest bikini and makeup bag and head back into the bathroom to get ready. I jump in the shower already planning how I'm going to do my hair and makeup. I'm going to look so hot that he won't be able to handle it, and then when I have him panting and begging me to forgive him, I'll break his heart by ignoring him and flirting with Chase's hot Navy SEAL friends.

I grin like an evil Bond villain as I turn on the hot water and let it wash away the dried sweat and stickiness from my skin. I feel better than ever.

This week won't be so bad if I get to watch Tucker squirming in jealousy.

In fact, it will be fucking awesome.

~

"Wow," a guy gasps as I walk by, looking hot as fuck. That gets him a smack from his wife.

I grin as I walk past them, thrusting my chest in the air as I strut to the beach. My black hair is done up, my makeup looks solid, and I'm wearing my tight Vix bikini. I look like Tucker's worst regret come to life: a young goofy girl that he loved to tease who then grew up into a goddess.

I stop at the beach bar for a drink, and although there's a crowd of tourists waiting to be served, the bartender comes straight to me. I look that good.

I let the other people pass first and then order a Long Island Ice Tea to bring down to the beach.

My girls are sitting on some beach chairs near the water with the rest of the wedding group.

"Mamma Mia!" Megan shouts, lowering her sunglasses to check me out as I walk toward them.

"Julia, you look stunning," Cynthia says, staring at me with her jaw hanging open. "Did you style your hair?"

"No," I lie. "I just fluffed it up a bit."

"You just fluffed it up a bit?" Megan repeats with a snort. "That's why you were in your room for over an hour? Just fluffing it up with your hand?"

I turn and glare at her. "Yes."

"Leave her alone," Tanya says, struggling to get out of the

beach chair to join us. "If you were single on a beach vacation with a bunch of hot Navy SEALS you would be doing the exact same thing."

"Lucky for me, I'm married," Megan says with a laugh, "and I don't have to do shit. It's a good fashion day for me when I'm not wearing a handkerchief in my hair like Aunt Jemima."

I take a sip of my drink as I look around the beach, looking for... Lucas. *Definitely* Lucas. Definitely not He-Who-Must-Not-Be-Named.

"Where's your husband?" I ask Megan. "I still haven't seen him."

Megan points to the volleyball game where Lucas is trying to keep up with the Navy SEALs. He's a tall lanky dentist who is as graceful as an ostrich on ice skates. He's playing on the same team as Ethan and Chase with a few other hot guys that I've never met. Lucas is the only one with his shirt on.

"They're just letting him play to be nice," Megan says, shaking her head as an easy lob bounces off his elbow.

The four of us watch the game with hungry eyes. It's like the best scene in Top Gun, but this time it's the live version. Eleven muscular shirtless men playing (and Lucas), all with a slick gleam of sweat on their hard muscles. I can hear *Playing with the Boys* playing in my head as I watch.

I've already forgotten all about Tucker. I take a quick look around, but I don't see him. *I wonder where he is.*

"So, what do we have here?" I ask Cynthia as I turn back to the game. "Who's the hottie in the red shorts?"

"That's Chuck," she says. "The guys call him Chucky."

"All right," I say grinning as my eyes roam over his hard chest and shredded abs. "Does Chucky want to get lucky?"

"I doubt it," Cynthia says, dousing the fire in my eyes. "He's married."

"Okay," I say with a sigh. "Chuck is out of luck. What about him? With the aviator sunglasses?"

Cynthia cringes. "Married with children."

Ugh.

I point out three more and in order they're engaged, married, and in a serious relationship. Megan can't stop laughing.

"Cynthia," I say, starting to panic. "Tell me there's at least one guy in there who isn't taken. *Please.*"

My best friend goes stiff and starts breathing heavy as she looks at one guy I haven't pointed out yet. He's not as hot as the others, but he's still muscular with a nice smile. I'll take anything at this point.

"Him? He's single?"

"Yeah," she mutters under her breath.

At least I have one option. "What's his name?"

"Greg," she says, biting her bottom lip. "But he's gay."

Megan snorts out a laugh beside me.

"What's so funny?" I snap, spinning on my heels as I glare at her.

She's turning red as she struggles to hold in her laughter. "You got all dressed up," she says in a cracking voice as her shoulders start to shake, "and they're all married." Her eyes are watering as she tries not to laugh in my face. "And the only one who's not, is gay." It's too much for her, and she bursts out laughing in front of me.

"Ugh," I say, shaking my head as Cynthia and Tanya start laughing as well.

"I'm sorry," Cynthia says, holding up her hand as she unsuccessfully tries to stop giggling. "It's not funny." She points at Megan as her body shakes with laughter. "*She's making me laugh.*"

I can't help but join in laughing with them, even though it's not funny and I hate every single one of them.

"I need another drink," I say with a sigh as I sit down on an empty beach chair.

"Good idea," Cynthia says, sitting down beside me. "Megan, you can go get them since you're part of the reason why Julia needs a drink."

"If I had to get a drink for everyone I drove crazy, I'd be a full-time waitress," she says, shaking her head as she turns.

"I'll go with you," Tanya says, following her. "I have to go pee again."

I take a deep breath as I look at the ocean in front of me. It's sparkling like there's a million diamonds floating on the surface. A seagull soars through the sky and lands in the sand next to a kid eating French Fries. If the bird had lips, he'd be licking them.

"Are you mad?" Cynthia asks, cringing as she turns to me.

"About what?" I ask, gritting my teeth as I stare forward. "The walking calendar of married guys over there or the fact that your brother is here and you didn't tell me?"

I turn to her with a glare, and she drops her eyes. I know it's her wedding week, but she should have warned me about her brother. She knows how I feel about him.

"I didn't know he was going to be here," she says, taking a deep breath before looking back up at me. "It was a surprise."

"What a great surprise," I say, rolling my eyes.

"It was for *me*," she snaps. "I'm sorry you two don't get along, but he's my brother, and I'm getting married this week. I'm really happy he's here."

I let out a breath as I watch my best friend. I guess I am being a little bit selfish. I should be happy that he's here for her. It is the most important week of her life.

"I'm sorry." I put my hand on hers and force out a smile. "We'll get along."

"Really?"

I nod as bile creeps up my throat. "It's going to be great."

"Thank you," she says as she leans over and gives me a hug. "We're all adults now. Maybe we can put all of that teenage stuff behind us."

"Totally."

She looks relieved and happy as she leans back on her chair. "Who knows? You two might even become friends."

"Maybe." I choke out the word as every cell in my body cringes.

Friends with Tucker? Never. I'd rather be friends with Stephanie, and that's saying a lot.

I'll act civil with him in front of Cynthia because it's her wedding week, but nothing is going to change between us.

He's still my enemy for life.

And I'm still going to make him pay.

CHAPTER THREE

DAY ONE

Tucker

How long does it take to put on a bikini?

I exhale in frustration as I lean on the bar beside the pool and order a beer. The two cute girls on the other end look over and smile when I meet their eyes. They're both sitting there in their bikinis, chewing on their straws as they fuck me with their eyes.

Normally, I would slide over there, introduce myself, and get this vacation started off right, but my mind is on something else at the moment. Some*one* else more precisely.

The bartender hands me the beer, and I reach into my bathing suit for a tip. I throw a couple bucks on the bar as I look around the pool area, trying to catch a glimpse of my sister's best friend. There are hot bodies everywhere, but not the one I want to see.

I smile and nod at the two girls as I take my beer and start walking around the resort. Feelings and emotions long buried come bubbling back up as I walk along the pool, sipping the cold beer. It's been over a decade since I left Buffalo to go live with my uncle, but when I saw Julia again, it was like no time at all had passed.

We picked up right where we left off: In the middle of an argument.

I laugh to myself as I remember how much I was in love with her back then and how I constantly screwed it all up.

I had a fucked-up way of showing my feelings, but it was the only way I knew how. I called her names, teased her, and tormented her. It's no wonder she still hates me.

Those juvenile tactics didn't work back then, and after seeing her storm off an hour ago, all frustrated and pissed off, it seems like they're not going to work this time either.

I was hoping to bury the hatchet with her on this trip and start over as friends, but our old way of jumping at each other's throats just kind of happened, and once we got going, it was too hard to stop. We slid into our old dysfunctional routine as easily as sliding into an old favorite jacket.

It was nice to see Cynthia. Seeing my sister reminds me that I have to visit Buffalo more often. Going back always reminds me of the painful time when I left, so I tend to avoid it. But I want to be closer to my little sister, and maybe her friend too, so I make a promise to myself to visit more.

My father had left us when Cynthia was still in diapers, and my mother was stuck raising us the best she could. As a kid, I didn't make it any easier on her, constantly getting into trouble at school and sometimes with the law. Growing up without a dad put a chip on my shoulder that steered me in the wrong direction. I desperately wanted to be a man, but with no male role model, I lost my way.

I don't blame my mother for sending me to live with my

uncle after I was brought home by the cops for stealing a bicycle, but it's still a painful memory for me. I was uprooted out of the only life I knew, the only town I'd ever been in, and sent to go live with Uncle Jack. Those first two years were the hardest. Uncle Jack was a military man, and his parenting tactics came straight out of boot camp. He whipped me into shape and was on my ass constantly until I started doing well in school, holding down a job, and molding me into the man I always wanted to be.

After high school, I made some good money planting trees up in Canada. It was hard work, but the pay was great, and I learned things that would later change my life. I was living in a camp deep in the forest, and the owner of the company took a liking to me. He taught me all about real estate investing, and when I got back home to Minneapolis, I took the money I had earned and bought my first piece of real estate. I made some money when I sold it a few years later, reinvested it, and four years later at age twenty-five, I had my first million in the bank. Another four years and a whole lot of hard work later, I'm worth almost ten.

I'm halfway done with my beer when I walk onto the beach and head to where the wedding group is sitting.

The groom and his friends are busy playing volleyball, and I keep my eye on Chase as I weave through the tourists relaxing on their beach chairs.

I'm not sure about this guy. He's too smooth. I know his type—the bad boy with the muscles and tattoos who charms the good girl with his soft words and seductive smile, only to cheat on her years later with a younger version. I know all about guys like him. I had a front row seat when I saw my father do it to my mother.

My body is rigid as I watch him. The ball comes flying towards him over the net, and he jumps up and smashes it down. The other team doesn't have a chance as it slams into the sand, leaving a deep crater where it landed.

He slaps hands with his friends, laughing as he playfully taunts the other team.

My muscles tense as he looks over at me and waves. I nod, but my face is unsmiling. Tight. Skeptical. I don't like this guy for my sister.

I turn away from my soon-to-be brother-in-law and loosen up when I see who's walking toward me.

"Hey, Tucker!" Megan says, waving as she approaches with Tanya. "Did you come to steal me away from my husband? Because I'll totally say yes."

I grin as we stop in front of each other. "I have a boat waiting for us," I say, flashing the girls my sexiest smile. "It's ready to bring us to a deserted island where we'll live beside a gorgeous lagoon, and I'll give you both foot massages every day for the rest of your lives."

"I'm in!" Megan says smiling up at me.

"Daily foot rubs do sound tempting," Tanya says with a shy smile. "But I'd probably sink the boat."

Megan wraps her hands around my arm and grins. "Looks like it's just us two!"

I glance over at the volleyball game, and Megan's husband is watching us with a look of concern on his face. "I think your husband is getting jealous," I whisper.

Megan sighs and then lets go of my arm. "Hi, honey!" she shouts as she waves to him. "You're looking great out there!"

Lucas' face breaks out into a big goofy grin as he turns back to the game, and almost immediately misses the ball.

"I'll see you guys back at the chairs," I say, walking past them.

"Just a warning," Tanya says. "Your old nemesis is there."

I nod to her and then turn with a grin on my face. *Perfect*.

I can hear the two of them whispering and giggling to each other as they walk away. Those two, Tanya and Megan, were always like putty in my hands. Growing up, I always wished that it was Julia who looked at me like that, but the only looks she ever gave me were filled with pure hatred.

I scan the beach chairs until I spot her. My heart starts thumping in my chest when I see her sitting next to my little sister. She's no longer the Julia from my childhood. She's a woman now.

And she's stunning.

Every nerve in my body stirs and tingles as I stand there, rooted to the spot like a statue. She's lying on a beach chair in only a tight black bikini that matches her flowing hair. Her full breasts are pouring out of her top, making me breathless as my hungry eyes devour every delectable inch of skin on her body.

I try not to think about how her ass must look in those tight bottoms because I'll get a hard-on in the middle of the beach.

My little sister's best friend is all grown up and has blossomed into the sexiest flower I have ever seen. I immediately regret every time I teased her, every name I called her, every time I pulled her hair as a child. It's like karma is real and the universe made her smoking hot just to fuck with me.

Well played, universe. Well played.

She laughs at something Cynthia says and the sight of her smile is so consuming that it makes me shiver. My chest tightens when she turns and spots me. The smile vanishes from her face, and she quickly turns away with a rigidness in that beautiful body of hers.

I swallow hard as I step forward, trying to clear the haze

from my mind. I can barely walk, so I have no idea how I'm going to put together a sentence in front of her. She's thrown me completely off my game.

"Hey, big brother!" Cynthia says, smiling up at me as I walk over. "We were just laughing at some of the old times. Weren't we all crazy back then? It's a good thing we're all grown up now and mature. Right, Tucker?"

"Right."

She turns to Julia with narrowed eyes. "Right, Julia?"

Julia's body is still stiff. *Stop looking at her body or something else is going to be stiff.*

"Right," she says in a tight voice.

"Great," Cynthia says, trying to put the past behind us. "Did you know that Tucker started his own business? A real estate investment company."

"That's interesting," Julia says. "The real estate prices must tank in whatever city you live in."

Cynthia frowns. "Tucker did you know that Julia is an elementary school teacher?"

I bet all the dads are fighting for the front row seats on parent teacher night.

"What grade?" I ask. I have a million questions for her. I want to know everything about her.

Julia scoffs. "Why? Are you interested in enrolling? Didn't you fail every class the first time around?"

Cynthia rolls her eyes. "She teaches kindergarten."

"The kids are pretty smart," Julia says. "I'm not sure if you'd get in."

Cynthia looks like she's about to chew us both out as my mother joins us, sitting beside me on the same beach chair.

"Did you guys see the video I posted on Facebook?" she asks as she stuffs her iPad into her beach bag.

"Mom, we're at the beach," Cynthia says, looking annoyed.

My mother doesn't seem to notice her daughter's frustration. "Well, you should watch it. Did you know that the Egyptian pyramids were actually made by ancient aliens? There's a whole documentary about it."

"Ancient aliens?" Cynthia asks as her shoulders drop. "You can't be serious."

My mother's brown curly hair bounces up and down as she nods her head. "It's true. You should watch it."

Cynthia has an incredulous look on her face as she stares at her. "Did *you* watch it?"

"No," she answers with a shrug. "But I read the headline. What? We're on the beach."

"I missed you, Mom," I say as Cynthia rolls her eyes. "Where else can I learn sci-fi history lessons?"

"Then come visit more," she says, grabbing my arm and pulling me into a sweaty side hug. "I miss you too."

"I don't," Julia mutters under her breath.

The volleyball game breaks up, and Chase's friends walk over to the ocean to cool off. Unfortunately, he doesn't join them.

Cynthia smiles as he walks over with a slight limp, spinning the ball on his finger. "Looking good out there, babe!" she says.

"I'm never as good without my partner by my side," he answers, sitting beside her with a smile on his face.

"You two like to play?" I ask.

"We play in a league every Tuesday night," Cynthia says proudly. "Two on two. We're undefeated."

"Beginner league?" I ask with a raised eyebrow.

Chase scoffs. "You saw my smash. Do you think I'm no good?"

My eyes narrow. "At volleyball or for my sister?"

"Tucker!" Cynthia snaps. "What the hell?"

I relieve the tension with a smile, but my eyes are still locked on him. "Just giving my little sister's boyfriend a hard time. That's what big brothers were made for."

"That's what you're made for?" Chase asks, not looking intimidated at all. He throws the ball at my chest, a little too hard. "Let's see what you're made *of*. Get a partner."

I squeeze the ball in my hands as he turns and charges off to the court.

"What was that for?" Cynthia asks with a sigh. "Can you try to be nice?"

"I am being nice," I say with a shrug as I get up. "We're going to play volleyball. It's going to be fun."

Cynthia shakes her head as she stands up. "Find a partner."

I turn and look down at the only girl in the world that I want as a partner. "Julia. Want to get sweaty?"

Cynthia grabs the ball out of my hands and tosses it in the air. "Go ask one of the guys in the water. Julia doesn't like to play."

But Julia's eyes are telling a different story. "I'll play," she says, standing up.

I swallow hard when I glance down at her body. Fuck, she looks good.

We walk to the court where Chase is pacing in the sand like a wild tiger. I seem to have gotten under his skin already. That was easy.

He eyes me as I set up on the other side of the net from him.

"Other side," Cynthia says, pointing at the net as she grabs Julia's hand. "Boys against the girls."

I hear Chase curse under his breath behind me. I guess he likes me as much as I like him.

"You two have to learn how to get along," Cynthia whispers as she walks up to me and stuffs the ball into my chest. "You get first serve."

I glance over at Julia who is looking nervous as Cynthia walks back to her, giving her a crash course in volleyball. At least I'll be facing her the entire game as she jumps and moves around in that tight bikini. I might even get to see a nip slip.

"Looks like it's you and me," I say to Chase as I duck under the net. He looks thrilled about that. "You serve first," I say, tossing him the ball.

I lock eyes on Julia as I set up in front. She gulps as she walks up to the net, looking like she just realized she made a horrible mistake.

"Don't worry, I'll go easy on you," I say as she stands in front of me.

"You've never gone easy on me before," she says with heated eyes. "Why start now?"

I grin as my eyes wander down her body. "Did you wear that bikini just to distract me? Smart move. It's working."

"Just keep your eyes on the ball, Mother Tucker," she snaps back. "You don't want to get beaten by a couple of girls, do you?"

"Service," Chase calls out as he spins the ball on his finger. "This one's got your name on it, babe."

My sister is all business as she stares back at her fiancée with a fierceness in her eye. She played volleyball all throughout high school and has always been a beast on the court.

"Quit yapping and send it over," she says, flexing her fingers and then squeezing them into fists.

Chase smiles as he tosses the ball up and smashes it, sending it flying in the corner beside his bride. Without a second of hesitation, Cynthia dives and smacks the ball with her wrist, sending it up in the air and keeping it in play.

Julia is better than I thought, and she quickly goes under it and lobs it up for Cynthia who is back on her feet. My sister comes leaping forward and spikes the ball down beside me before I can even react.

"Nice!" Julia shouts, giving her a high five as they celebrate.

"Who's the beginner here?" Chase mutters behind me.

I shake my head as I loosen up. They caught me off guard on that one, but it won't happen again.

"Why are you looking so upset?" Julia says, taunting me through the net. "Did you get sand in your vagina?"

I take a deep breath and try to ignore her as Cynthia gets ready to serve. "I'm torn, Chase," she says as she shakes her head. "I want to smash it in your face, but I don't want my groom to have a black eye for the wedding."

"You're welcome to try if you think you can get it over here with that weak little serve of yours," he replies, taunting her back.

Cynthia grins and then tosses the ball up. She hits it with a grunt, and it flies like a rocket over the net and over my head. Chase is faster than I gave him credit for, and he dives with his arm out, hitting the ball up before it hits the sand.

I run over to the ball and hit it, but it flies straight into the net.

My face reddens as Julia and Cynthia start laughing at me.

"Come on, man," Chase grunts as he gets up. His chest is covered in sand. "Even Julia hit the ball. No offense, Julia."

Julia is laughing at me. "Yeah, Tucker. Even *I* hit the ball."

"I hit the ball," I mutter to myself. "It just didn't go over the fucking net."

We keep playing, and I start to get better as I loosen up. It's been years since I last played volleyball, but I'm starting to get the hang of it again. It's a tight game, and the score is tied.

Tanya and Megan are watching from the sidelines, rooting for the girls and taunting us.

"Hit it with your purse next time!" Megan shouts when Chase hits the ball and it goes out of bounds.

He just shakes his head.

The girls rotate positions, and Julia comes up to the front of the net while Cynthia gets ready to serve.

"Your nipple is showing," I say to her as Cynthia throws the ball up and hits it over.

Julia gasps and looks down at her incredible tits as I jump up and smack the ball down beside her, getting us a point.

"No fair," she whines as she bends over and picks up the ball.

I swallow hard as I glance down at her black bikini bottoms covering the dick-hardening curves of her perfect ass.

"They have to cheat to win," Tanya says, shaking her head. "Pathetic."

I grin at Julia as she tosses me the ball. "All is fair in love and volleyball."

"That's how you want to play it?" she asks with a nod. "All right."

I laugh as I walk to the back of the court and step behind

the rope. I have one eye on Julia, who is bent over with the tops of her beautiful tits hanging out of her bikini, as I throw the ball up to serve it. She's too distracting, and I flub the ball, hitting it straight into the net.

"Oh, come on!" Chase complains, throwing his hands in the air.

"My bad," I mumble as the girls celebrate on the other side of the court.

"Looks like those big muscles are only for show," Julia says, laughing at me. "Are they inflatable?"

"Why, you want to blow me?" I ask with a grin.

"Actually, I'd be more interested in deflating you," she says with a glare. "Deflating your ego, your heightened sense of importance, and then finally your lungs."

"Enough yapping," Chase says as he throws the ball to his bride. "We're down two points."

"Yeah, Chase," Julia repeats with a smug look on her gorgeous face. "You're down two points. Get your head in the game."

She's teasing me, but she's right. My mind has been on her this entire time. But how could it not be with her looking like *that* in front of me?

A few minutes later and the game is almost over. Cynthia is about to serve, and if the girls get this point, they win.

Chase is pacing behind me, looking stressed out. I didn't realize he was so competitive, but then again, I guess every Navy SEAL is.

Julia is standing in front of me looking absolutely delicious. Her skin has a sheen of sweat on it with little flecks of sand sprinkled all over. I want to call a time out just so I can stare at her until the sun goes down.

"You look nervous," she says, blinking at me with those lush, sexy lashes. I almost get hard on the spot. "Afraid you're going to lose to a bunch of girls?"

"Focus," Chase warns me.

I just ignore him. "My partner wants me to focus," I whisper to her. "That's impossible with your tight body in front of me, looking like that. I think that bikini should be against the rules. It's an unfair advantage."

"You shouldn't be talking about unfair," she says with a huff. "Especially to *me*."

"Service!" Cynthia yells as she tosses the ball up. She smacks it over the net, and Chase rushes under it. He lobs it up and I hit it back over.

Cynthia dives and keeps the ball in play. Julia runs over and hits it back over to us.

Chase nails it back to Cynthia who hits it off her forearm. She gets lucky with the hit and it comes flying up high on my side. I grin, holding my hands up as I watch it flying up in the air. It's going to be an easy spike.

Just as I'm about to leap up and spike it down, Julia grabs the waistband of my bathing suit with both hands and yanks it down my legs.

Tanya, Megan, Cynthia, Julia, and half the beach burst out laughing as my bathing suit shoots down to my ankles, exposing my cock to half the resort.

The volleyball falls to the sand as I grab my bathing suit and yank it back up my legs.

"Girls win!" Megan shouts as Julia and my sister jump up and down, celebrating.

"What the hell?" I shout with my arms open.

Julia turns with a grin on her flushed face. "All is fair in love and volleyball," she says with her eyes sparkling. "You said so yourself!"

I grin as she marches away in celebration with her friends. My eyes are on her tight little ass as they head to the beach bar for a celebratory drink.

So, we both played unfair in volleyball. Let's see how we play in love.

CHAPTER FOUR

DAY ONE

Julia

If this doesn't get his heart racing, then I don't know what will.

I grin as I look myself up and down in the mirror. *Perfect.* I'm wearing a short silver Alexander McQueen dress that will bring him to his knees. I hope so, it cost me a month's salary.

Maybe *three* months after I count the credit card interest added up on it.

But still, it will all be worth it if it drives He-Who-Must-Not-Be-Named crazy. I want him to fall madly in love with me so he can go to his grave regretting how he treated me for all those years.

I'm wearing my hair up tonight, and my tanned shoulders look sexy with the spaghetti straps of the designer dress. I take one last look and then head out of my room to the resort's seafood restaurant where the wedding group are all having dinner together.

I step into the hallway and drop my head in frustration

when I see who my neighbor is. Tucker is walking out of his door as well. The door right next to mine.

"You're my neighbor?" I ask, shaking my head in disbelief. "I knew this room was too good to be true."

"It is good," he says with a grin that makes my pulse race. "Now I don't have to run too far for any late-night booty calls. You can just knock on the wall, and I'll be right over."

My heart is pounding as I try to convince myself that I won't be lying awake at night thinking of any booty calls. He laughs as I glare at him.

When he turns to make sure his door is locked, I quickly look him up and down, checking out every inch of his huge frame. He's wearing gray shorts and a tight black t-shirt that hugs his round muscles. His tattoos look sexier than ever creeping down his thick arms, and I have to hold my hands firmly at my sides so they don't reach out and touch them.

He looks even hotter in the soft lighting of the hallway than he did on the beach, if that's possible. His skin has some color from the sun, which makes his honey-colored eyes look even more intense. They're locked on me as he slowly looks me up and down.

"Wow," he says in a breathless tone. "That dress was made for you."

"Thank you," I mutter as I close the door. I pretend like his compliment means nothing to me, but I'm holding back a smile.

"I thought you couldn't beat that black bikini, but fuck," he says, shaking his head as his sexy eyes roam over me.

"Now I know why this room was empty in the first place," I say, rolling my eyes as I start walking down the hall. He jogs to catch up to me. "Nobody could handle the obnoxious fumes coming out of your mouth."

"I think it was fate," Tucker says with a smile.

"I don't think fate is that cruel," I say, quickening my pace.

"Why are you walking so fast?" he asks as he keeps pace with me. "Excited to get this night over with so we can get that booty call started?"

I stop and spin on my Sophia Webster heels, sticking my finger in Tucker's face as I glare at him. "There will be no booty calls. Got that? There will be no calls of any kind. If I haven't made myself perfectly clear already, then let me explain. I. Don't. Like. You."

He just stands there grinning, which makes me hate him even more.

"You were horrible to me when we were kids, and just because you grew up to be hot doesn't change all of that."

"You think I'm hot?"

"Ugh!" I throw my hands in the air and storm away from him. He's the most frustrating man on the planet. I shouldn't have said that word, but it just kind of slipped out. I'm not as sharp as I usually am when I'm around Tucker. His heart-racing smile and intoxicating smell seem to dull my common sense.

"How hot?" he asks as he follows me. "A ten? A ten point five?"

"How about we talk about your personality? Because that gets a zero."

"What about my cock?"

My breath catches in my throat, and I almost forget to keep walking when I think about his long beautiful cock hanging down between his legs. It definitely gets a ten.

Ten inches.

"I didn't look," I say, keeping my eyes and my flushing cheeks forward. "Not interested."

"Well, I'm right next door if you change your mind."

"I won't."

He chuckles. "We'll see about that."

I whip my head around, about to lay into him when his mother comes walking up to us. "Hey, guys!" she says, holding up her iPad. "You two look beautiful. Let's get a quick picture."

I cringe just thinking about it. "I think we're running late, Mrs. Connor. We should just go ins—"

Tucker wraps his warm muscular arm around my bare shoulder and pulls me into his side. His soft hand on my shoulder mixed with his musky cologne is making my nipples hard. And I hate him for it.

"Flash that beautiful smile of yours," he whispers as his mother raises the iPad over her face. "You don't need your flash, Mom. Julia's smile lights up the whole resort."

"Say cheese," Mrs. Connor says.

"I'll say *cheese* to that," I whisper as I try to lean away from him. "Because that was the cheesiest line I've ever heard."

Cynthia's mother takes the picture, and I dart away from Tucker while his mother waves him over to see the photo.

"Where are you going?" he calls out to me.

I turn and glare at him over my shoulder. "I want to get a good seat. The one furthest from you."

He chuckles as he walks over to his mother to see the picture that she's proudly holding up. "Can you send that to me?" I hear him ask his mother as I charge away.

Megan and Lucas pop out of nowhere, scaring the dirty thoughts out of me.

"I hope you brought your running shoes," Megan says, grabbing my arm. "Because we're ripping up the dance floor tonight with our synchronized dance."

"No, we're not," I say, shaking my head.

"Did you get the email I sent with the updated moves?" she asks, ignoring me. "Have you been practicing?"

I turn to see if she's joking but unfortunately, she's serious.

"You brought running shoes?" I ask. I shouldn't be shocked. Megan brings running shoes whenever she goes dancing. I think she tries to look as ridiculous as possible on purpose.

"Lucas has them."

I turn and look back at her tall husband who is following us. He's got her running shoes tucked under his arm. He just shrugs when I look at them.

"Why do you encourage her?" I ask.

He smiles at his wife. "I love watching her dance."

"Well, that makes one in eight billion," I say, laughing at her.

"*Two*, in eight billion," Megan says, raising two fingers. "I love watching myself dance as well."

I laugh as I squeeze her hand with my arm. "Why am I not surprised?"

We get to the restaurant, and the bride and groom are already there. Cynthia and Chase reserved a long table for the group, so we all sit together. Tanya and Ethan arrive as we sit down, and so does Tucker and his mom. I sit beside Cynthia with Tanya and Ethan in front of me. Tucker and his mother sit in front of me to the side. It takes some effort, but I keep my eyes off of him no matter how many times I see him glancing at me through my peripheries.

"So, Tanya," I say, turning away from him. "How is the new place?"

She and Ethan moved from Chicago back to Buffalo a few months ago, and they just bought a house. Ethan is a tattoo artist, and he's in the middle of setting up a new shop.

"There are boxes everywhere," she says, looking flustered.

"It's just temporary," Ethan says, placing a comforting hand on hers. "We'll get it all done. We're just focusing on setting up the tattoo shop first."

He goes on about the tattoo shop, discussing it with his brother as I nod my head, pretending to listen. I'm more interested in what Cynthia and Tucker are talking about, so I eavesdrop on them.

"What happened with the girlfriend?" Cynthia asks him. "I thought you and Stacy were getting along?"

"We were," he says with a laugh, "until I found out she was crazy."

Cynthia scoffs. "Guys love to call women crazy, but it's usually the guy's fault that they're acting that way in the first place."

"Not this one," Tucker says with a laugh. "This girl was legitimately, certifiably crazy. She was too good to be true at first, but eventually I realized she was just that—too good to be true."

"Are you sure you're not being too hard on her?" their mother Amy asks.

"Nope. She was sweet at first, but then the charade started to slip away. A homeless man touched her leg when we were walking home from dinner, and she kicked him in the ribs."

"Sounds like a winner," Mrs. Connor says.

"Sounds like someone we know," Cynthia says with a laugh. I know just who she's talking about—Lucas' sister Stephanie. She is a train wreck of a person who tried to ruin both Megan's and Tanya's weddings, but we got her back.

Last I heard about her, she was stuck in a prison cell in Belize for smacking a few cops.

"Do you think that's a good idea, Julia?" Ethan asks.

I'm staring right at him, but I haven't been listening to a word he has said for the past five minutes. I start to panic as Tanya, Chase, Ethan, Megan, and Lucas all stare at me, waiting for me to answer.

"Great idea," I say with a gulp. I have a fifty-fifty shot to answer correctly.

And by the frown on Tanya's face, I apparently chose wrong.

"See?" Ethan says to Tanya. "Julia thinks it's a good idea."

Tanya looks at me with pure betrayal written across her face. "I can't believe you think that Rocko is a good name for our son."

Is it rude to crawl under the table?

I picture myself doing it and then cringe when my mind goes to a dirty place. Because the first place I picture myself going while on my knees is straight to Tucker to take that big delicious cock out of his pants.

I raise my hand to the waitress. "Can I get a drink, please? A strong one."

Something tells me I'm going to be uttering those words a lot this week.

This is the part I've been dreading the most.

But now that we're finally doing it, I'm having a lot of fun. *Everybody* by the Backstreet Boys is blaring through the speakers as Megan, Cynthia, me, and a very pregnant Tanya are doing our synchronized dance that we made up for a high school talent show. We weren't very good back then, and we're totally laughable right now.

I know this because everyone is laughing at us. But that's okay because we're laughing even harder than them.

Cynthia crashes into me, nearly sending me flying to the ground as we start the grand finale. Megan's face looks so intense as she flies around the dance floor in her running shoes. Tanya looks exhausted as she stands in one spot, waving her arms.

I try to keep my eyes off of Tucker, but it's hard. I steal one quick glance and then blush when I see him smiling at me. He seems to be enjoying the show, but then again, who doesn't like to watch a car crash?

We awkwardly shake our hips and throw our hands in the air for the grand finale, and when the music cuts, the place goes crazy. And by crazy, I mean people in our wedding group clap and cheer, but everyone else in the bar just looks happy we're done.

"Please don't make me do that again," I say to a sweaty Megan as she high fives us.

"You have a ten-minute break, and then we're doing Spice Girls," she says, rolling her shoulders as she gets ready for round two.

I'm about to protest, but she runs to the bar before I can say a word. Probably to rehydrate with a couple of bottles of water after her intense dancing.

"I'm so proud of you guys," Mrs. Connor says. "And I got the whole thing on video!"

Cynthia turns to her with heated eyes. "Mom, if you put that on Facebook, I'll murder you."

"Too late!" she says, hurrying away.

Cynthia runs after her mother to try and wrestle the

iPad out of her hands while Tanya takes a deep breath. "I'm going to go sit down," she says. "My feet are killing me."

He-Who-Must-Not-Be-Named is watching me from the bar, so I turn and walk the other way, heading outside for some air.

The resort looks beautiful at night with the soft lighting of the pool and the bright stars overhead. There's a cool breeze that feels nice on my hot skin. I take a deep breath as I walk to the beach. I'm in so much debt that I don't know when I'll ever get to be on a beach again. I have to enjoy it while I can.

I slip out of my Sophia Webster heels and let my toes sink into the cool powdery sand as the waves hit the shore in a soft rhythm. I'm in so much debt that it might take decades for me to pay it off. That thought makes me want to bury my head in the sand forever.

"That was some interesting dancing in there," Tucker says from behind me.

I turn with a start. "Megan has a temper tantrum whenever we deny her. It's just easier this way."

"Well, you looked amazing back there," he says, swallowing hard as he looks me up and down. "And you look even more incredible now."

I could say the same about him. He looks stunning with the soft light of the moon lighting up his gorgeous face and broad shoulders. He'd be perfect to cuddle up next to on one of these beach chairs and gaze up at the stars with. Ya know, if he wasn't such a fucking asshole.

He stops next to me and looks out at the ocean. "Are you going cliff jumping tomorrow?" he asks.

Cynthia planned a few group activities throughout the week. Our first one tomorrow is cliff jumping. We're going on a forty-minute hike to an area of the island with high cliffs, and then for some reason, we have to jump off them. I don't get it either.

"I'm going," I say. Not by choice. Cynthia paid for my ticket before asking me about it. "Are you?"

"I am," he says, flashing me those sexy white teeth. My heart starts thumping as I look up at them. "You've been telling me to jump off a cliff for years, so I thought I'd give it a try."

I laugh. "You should practice tonight and jump off your balcony."

"I'd never make it to the pool."

I grin. "I know."

He smiles and then his face goes still. "I want to get serious for a second," he says.

"I'm already being serious," I say with a straight face. "You should totally dive off your balcony."

He ignores my comment. "What's up with Chase?"

I look up at him and exhale. "He loves your sister. She loves him. They're great for each other, and you shouldn't make things difficult for them during their wedding week. That's what's up."

"The last thing I want to do is make things difficult for my sister during her wedding week, but I don't know about him. I know his type."

"What's his type?"

"Cocky. Arrogant. Thinks he's God's gift to women."

I laugh as I stare him in the eyes. "I wonder how you would know his type so well."

He shakes his head. "This is serious. She's my little sister."

"She's not little anymore," I say. "Cynthia is a smart, sophisticated woman. She can make her own decisions."

He sighs as he looks away from me and stares at the ocean. "I don't know."

I step in front of him and glare at him. "Well, I *do* know. He's a great guy. Give him a chance."

"We'll see."

I stick my finger in his face and grit my teeth. Cynthia is my best friend, and she's found an amazing guy who makes her happy. I'll be damned if I'm going to let anyone, even her brother, ruin that for her.

"Don't fuck this up for her," I hiss. "If you think we're enemies now, you haven't seen nothing if you do anything to ruin her week."

He shows me his palms as he steps back. "I'm not going to do anything. I'm just worried about my little sister."

I take a deep breath and then exhale slowly, trying to calm my raging nerves. He's just doing what any good big brother is supposed to do: look after his sister.

"Just give him a chance, okay," I say, much calmer now. "He's different than what you think you know. I think you'll like him if you give him a real chance."

He nods as he looks down at me. "I'll give him a chance if you give me a chance."

I jerk my head back in surprise.

"I'm different than what you think you know," he says with a softness on his face and in his voice. "I think you'll like me if you give me a real chance."

He gives me a shy smile before turning and walking back to the bar.

I take a deep breath of the cool Caribbean air as I turn back toward the ocean with his words swirling around in my head.

Give He-Who-Must-Not-Be-Named another chance?

I gulp as my chest tightens. But what if I like what I see?

CHAPTER FIVE

Julia

I stare at my ringing cell phone with an empty feeling in the pit of my stomach. My mouth is dry as I stare at the *Blocked Number* showing on the screen.

I woke up half an hour ago to the sun shining without a cloud in the sky. I felt great as I made some coffee and sat on the balcony, watching the turquoise waves roll onto the beach.

And now this.

These guys always ruin my day.

I should just let it go to voicemail, but for some reason I pick it up.

"Hello?"

"*Is this Julia Tanner?*"

I gulp. "Yes."

"*This is Richard calling from The Wellington Collection Agency. I'm calling about an outstanding debt that you have with us.*"

This is a new one. I've been getting calls from Smith and Sons Collectors, the Samuel Group, and the Marion Debt Payment Group, but I've never heard of the Wellington Collection Agency.

"*You owe us seventeen thousand, six hundred and twelve dollars,*" he says.

I look in the mirror and watch as my face goes pale. That's another seventeen thousand added to my tab of seventy-six thousand. I'm glad I don't have a calculator on me or I would throw up.

"*How would you like to pay?*"

"I would like to pay with money, but I don't have any."

He doesn't sound happy. "*Then I guess we'll be over this afternoon to repossess all of your stuff.*"

He's a little late for that. The Samuel Group already emptied out my closet. I had to hide these clothes in Cynthia's garage.

"*You have one week to pay what you are owing in full, or we'll be forced to sue you.*"

"I'm a kindergarten teacher," I say, starting to panic. "How am I supposed to get seventeen thousand dollars in a week?"

"*Steal your student's lunch money if you have to,*" he says. "*That's not my problem. You have one week.*"

The phone clicks dead, and I drop down on the bed as nausea creeps up my throat. I'm so fucked.

I'll be paying my debt until I'm eighty. I'll never be able to retire, and what's worse is no man will want to be with me if I have six figures in debt following me around like a weighted ball.

I close my eyes as I lie on my back, trying to calm the raging butterflies in my stomach.

My phone rings again, and without thinking, I answer it.

"Hello?"

"*May I speak to Julia?*"

I exhale in relief. Debt collectors are never this polite.

"This is her."

"*Hi, I'm calling from the Fitness Unlimited Gym. Unfortunately, your credit card has been declined for the past two months in a row. Do you have an active card that we can put on file?*"

I squeeze my eyes shut, trying to keep from crying. "No. I'm all out of credit cards." My mother cut them into plastic confetti.

"*Well, then unfortunately we're going to have to cancel your membership,*" the voice says.

"Okay," I say, trying to keep my chin from quivering. "I understand."

The woman hangs up, and I turn off my phone before my hairdresser calls and tells me that I owe her all of my hair.

"Oh, Julia," I mutter as I cover my eyes with my hands. "What have you done?"

I turn around, stuff my face into the pillow, and cry.

"Who's ready to jump off a cliff?" Cynthia asks when I walk into the lobby. We're all supposed to meet at eight thirty in the lobby, but He-Who-Must-Not-Be-Named is not here.

Maybe he took my advice from last night and jumped off his balcony.

I grin at the thought, but unfortunately, he comes strutting in a minute later looking hotter than ever in his board shorts with palm trees on them, and a white tank top. His arms and chest look massive in his tight top. For a second, I imagine how his big arms would feel wrapped around me before I catch myself and turn away with a light head.

He walks straight toward me, but it's too early to deal with him. I'm still upset from the calls this morning, so I head to the safety of my friends rather than let him add to my agitation. I always feel better surrounded by the security of my fellow lionesses.

"I'm so happy that I'm pregnant and don't have to do this," Tanya says with a big smile on her face. Tanya is not too adventurous, and she'd much rather be watching from the boat.

Chase's Navy SEAL friends are hanging around by the fountain near us, looking excited for the excursion. "At least you're going to have a great view," I say, grinning at her.

She leans in with red cheeks. "Pregnancy has made me so horny," she whispers. "I saw a cucumber at the buffet yesterday and got turned on. This is going to be too much."

Megan laughs. "You're turning into your Aunt Ophelia. I knew it was inevitable."

"I hope Ethan is *rising* to the challenge," Cynthia says with a giggle.

"Oh, he is," she says with a nod. "But I'm starting to tire him out. I've been craving sex twenty-four-seven the past month. Is that normal?"

"For someone turning into Aunt Ophelia it is," Megan says with a grin.

"It's better than the alternative," I whisper. "I haven't gotten any in months." I've been way too stressed out to think about sex with all of my debt problems. And besides, where am I supposed to bring a guy home to? My parent's basement?

We all get on the bus, and I make an effort to stay clear

of Tucker. He sits with his mother in the back as I squeeze in next to Tanya. Megan and Cynthia are sitting behind us.

After about an hour of Tanya and Megan trying to get everyone on the bus to sing along to over a dozen songs, we arrive.

"Remind me never to sit next to those two again," I whisper to Cynthia as we get out with our ears ringing.

She laughs. "I think I saw room in the trunk underneath the bus."

"That sounds like paradise," I say with a laugh. "We'll hide in there on the way back."

After we meet the guide, we begin the beautiful hike through the rainforest that leads to the cliffs. A lush canopy of gleaming leaves covers our heads as we walk along the worn path full of thick, twisting tree roots and sharp rocks. Monkeys are shrieking in the distance, and I look around for them but only see a scattering of colorful tropical birds singing on the large tree branches. The air is thick with heat, and it smells natural, like rotting vegetation. I'd much prefer a shopping mall, but this is okay too.

It takes Tucker less than five minutes to worm his way up beside me.

"I waited all night for a knock," he says, grinning at me as he matches my stride. "What happened?"

"And I waited all night to hear the splat from you jumping off your balcony," I answer back. "What happened there?"

He smiles. "Are you ever going to forgive me for what happened when we were kids?"

I narrow my eyes on him. "Are you ever going to apologize?"

"I'm sorry," he says.

"Not accepted."

He shakes his head. "Big surprise."

My heart starts hammering in my chest as I remember all of the things he did to me. "You were such a jerk to me *for years*, and I'm just supposed to let it all go because you say two simple words? I don't think so."

"I wasn't *that* bad," he says with a shrug.

My body tenses as I turn to him with a clenched jaw. He can act like he's changed all he wants to, but I'll be damned if he thinks what he put me through wasn't *that bad*.

"You made fun of me when I fell off my bike and scratched my knee," I say, glaring at him. "You hit me and pulled my hair more times than I can remember. You called me names like Mosquito Bites and Julia Fool-ia. You tormented me for years. I hated you."

A flush creeps up his neck and cheeks as he listens with a cringing face.

"You broke my recorder in the seventh grade," I say, getting angrier as all the horrible memories come flooding back. "You stole my book report in grade three and tossed it in the sewer. You made fun of every pimple that I had. You made me cry more times than everyone else in my life combined. I hated you. I still hate you. And I will *always* hate you. Now please, fuck off!"

I storm ahead with heat ripping through my tense body. I'm grinding my teeth so hard that my jaw hurts as I charge up the path, leaving him behind me in my past where he belongs.

When I can't take it anymore and finally turn to look back at him, I'm shocked to see him looking upset. His head is lowered as he shuffles along the path, looking embarrassed and full of regret.

I whip my head back around and stare forward with a

clenched jaw. *Don't feel sorry for him. He deserves more than that.*

This has been an all round shitty morning, and I just want to be by myself. I walk ahead of the group for a while, ignoring the beautiful lush rainforest around me, cursing the insatiable debt collectors, cursing the old Julia who couldn't control herself with a small piece of plastic, but most of all, cursing out Tucker. I hate that he's here, I hate that his presence is dragging up old painful memories that have been long forgotten, but most of all, I hate that all I want to do is slide my hands up under his shirt as I kiss his soft lips every time I look at him.

It makes me furious. *He* makes me furious.

I'm actually excited to jump off that cliff. Maybe I'll get lucky and land right in a great white shark's hungry mouth.

About twenty minutes later, when I've finally calmed down, he comes walking up beside me.

"What?" I snap, staring straight ahead. "If I didn't make myself clear before, I don't want you anywhere near me."

"Oh, you made it clear," he says in a soft voice. "I just wanted to give you a proper apology."

I cross my arms and shake my head as I quicken my pace. "I don't want to hear it."

He speeds up, staying by my side. "I *am* sorry, Julia," he says with a sigh. "I feel horrible for making your life difficult. I was young and *very* stupid. I had a weird way of showing that I liked you."

His words are like a punch in the gut. I can't breathe. I'm seeing stars. "What was that?" I choke out. "*You* liked *me*?"

He looks as shocked as I feel. "I thought that was obvious."

"That was anything but obvious," I say, staring up at him in disbelief. "I thought you hated me."

His head jerks back like I slapped him. "I was in love with you. I was obsessed with you."

My mind is racing. I close my eyes and shake my head, trying to clear the jumbled thoughts, but nothing is adding up. He was in love with me? Tucker? With me?

"Are you sure?" I ask, staring at him with a tightness in my chest.

He chuckles. "I'm sorry, Julia. I wish I had taken a different approach to showing you how I felt, but like I said, I was young and *very* stupid. I was afraid of my feelings, so I did the opposite of what I wanted. I guess I rejected you before you could reject me."

"You did a lot more than reject me," I say, taking a deep breath. "You made my life a living hell."

He lowers his head and sighs. "I wish I could make it up to you."

I cross my arms and look straight ahead. "You can't."

I quicken my pace again, but this time he stays back. I'm disgusted with myself that I'm sad that he does.

He's your nemesis. Just because he's hot doesn't excuse him for all the shit he put you through. Don't fall for his game.

A few minutes later, we arrive at the cliffs. "Oh, shit," I gasp when I look over them. They're higher than I thought.

The wind is fierce and unforgiving as it smashes into me, making my hair whip around. My stomach drops as I inch toward the edge and peek down at the deep water below.

Tanya is sitting in a boat that is there to pick us up from the rough ocean after we jump. She looks like a little minnow from this height.

"Holy shit!" Megan says, swallowing hard as she joins me at the edge. "We need parachutes to jump off this thing."

Cynthia's face turns white when she joins us. "I'm going to die before my wedding," she says, looking paralyzed with fear as she peeks over. "It didn't look this high up in the brochure."

Chase's Navy SEAL friends look excited as they take off their shoes and tie the laces around their arms. They're used to more dangerous things than this. This is as relaxing as a spa day to a Navy SEAL.

One by one, they start leaping off the cliff, doing flips and spins and other moves that have us wanting to puke with worry.

They all land in the water and swim to the boat, laughing like they didn't just risk their lives for a few seconds of fun.

Chase and Ethan approach the edge, grinning as they look over the deadly cliff from hell.

"That's high," Chase says with a laugh. "You girls can walk back if you want."

"Can I walk back too?" Ethan asks with a gulp.

Chase grins at him. "No way. You're jumping."

Ethan looks up at the sky, says a quick prayer, then runs and jumps off with a howl.

My stomach drops as I watch him sail through the air like Superman and then land feet first with a huge splash.

"I'm not doing that," Megan says, shaking her head. "Fuck this."

She looks up at her husband Lucas, who is shaking in his flip flops. "I better walk her back," he says with a gulp. They both hurry back down the path before anyone can make fun of them.

Chase grins as he looks at Cynthia. "What are you thinking?"

Cynthia's jaw is clenched as she stares down at the water. The harsh wind is whipping her curly brown hair around. "I'm thinking I want to follow Megan and Lucas back," she says. "But I'm also thinking that this is my wedding week and a perfect time to jump into things with both feet."

Chase holds out his hand and grins. "That's my girl."

She takes a deep breath and then slaps her hand into his. "On three."

The bride and groom kiss each other on the lips and then count. "One. Two. *Three*."

My heart stops as the two of them leap over the cliff while holding hands. They land in the water down below with a huge splash, and I don't take a breath until their heads pop out a few seconds later.

"I can't," I say, turning to catch up with Megan. Instead I crash right into Tucker's hard chest.

"Not jumping?" he asks.

I shrug. "I don't feel like dying today, so..."

"Okay," he says, walking past me. "I'll see you at the bus."

I take a few steps and then stop. "Are you jumping?" I ask, turning around.

He nods. "Look," he says before taking a deep breath. "If I die right now, I want to die with a clear conscience. I don't expect you to forgive me, but I want you to know that I'm—"

I raise my hand, shutting him up. "I don't want to hear it. You don't get to have a clear conscience after what you put me through. Got it?"

"Julia," he says, locking eyes on me. "I'm telling you. I'm—"

"Fuck this," I mutter and just start running. I don't know why I do it, but I just can't stand to be around this guy for a second longer.

I sprint with all my might to the edge of the cliff and leap over with my arms and legs flailing.

I regret it as soon as my feet leave the ground.

My stomach is in my throat as I plummet down to the water with the wind whipping me violently. I'd scream until I pass out, but the air is ripped from my lungs, and I can't make a sound.

A million thoughts race through my head, but I have a moment of clarity right before I slam into the water. One thought stands out.

I've always loved Tucker too.

The thought is as jarring as my landing. I slam into the water with a force that knocks the wind out of me. I rocket down into the depths of the ocean like a torpedo and don't stop until the water is freezing cold and my head feels like it's about to explode from the pressure.

I frantically kick my legs and swim up as my chest burns for oxygen. My head starts to get light as I run out of the air that it desperately needs. I kick and kick and kick as I force my mouth to stay closed. It's demanding me to open it and take in a breath of air, but all it's going to get is a mouthful of seawater.

Finally, my head pops out of the water, and I take the most glorious breath of air I've ever had. My arms and legs feel like heavy weights as I look around for the boat.

Oh no.

It's too far away. The waves are picking up, and it's drifted so far. Too far...

I can barely keep my head above water as my wet clothes and heavy shoes weigh me down. The tide starts taking me away from the boat, and I'm too weak to fight it.

I try to call for help, but I get a mouthful of sea water instead.

And then...

I start sinking.

CHAPTER SIX

DAY TWO

Tucker

Oh, thank God.

I can finally take a breath of relief when Julia's head pops out of the water. My heart nearly stopped with worry when I saw her leap over the cliff.

But she's not out of trouble yet. She's far from the boat, and the strong waves are pushing her farther with every passing second.

Adrenaline courses through my veins when her head dunks under the rough water and her arms start flailing. She's in trouble.

I leap off the cliff without a second of hesitation, diving down to save her. The water can't come fast enough as I squeeze my hands into fists, bracing myself for the impact.

As soon as I slice through the water, I curve my body and swim in her direction as fast as I can, praying that I'm not too late. When my lungs are burning for air, I come out of the water, frantically looking for her. *There!* I see her a few yards away. She's not looking good.

There's a panicked look in her eyes, and her mouth is wide open as a wave hits the back of her head, plunging her back down.

I can see to my right that a couple of the Navy SEALs are swimming over, trying to get to her as well.

I grit my teeth and kick as hard as I can, ripping through the water to get to the only girl I've ever loved.

Her body is in pure panic mode when I reach her. She tries to lunge on me, and her fist slams into my nose.

"Easy," I say to her as I swim around to her back. "Just relax."

She's past listening. She's drowning, and her instinct has taken over, trying to grab onto anything and everything to keep her head from going under.

When I see an opening, I swoop in and slide my arms around her waist, squeezing her tight.

"Stop moving," I whisper in her ear as I hold her up. "It's okay, Julia. I got you. I won't let anything happen to you."

Her body finally stops thrashing around, and I lean back, holding her with one arm and swimming back to the rocks with the other.

Two Navy SEALs arrive, and I wave them off. "I got her," I tell them. "Bring the boat over to the cliff and pick us up."

They both nod, turn, and swim back to the boat.

My hand hits a flat rock, and I climb up onto it, carefully pulling Julia up with me. She's looking pale as I lie her down on her back.

"You're okay now," I whisper to her. Her tilted head is resting on my right hand, and I'm combing her black hair out of her face with my left. She's the most beautiful thing

I've ever seen. This is a horrible moment for her, but for me, it's one of the best of my life. I wish it would last forever.

Suddenly, her eyes bulge out and she jerks up to a sitting position. She starts dry heaving and then pukes salt water all over herself.

"It's okay," I whisper as I ease her back down to the rock. "You swallowed some salt water. That's all it is."

I scoop up some water from the ocean and gently wash it off her body. She finally comes back to normal, looking up at me with life in her eyes.

I hold her close as we gaze into each other's eyes, seeing something that wasn't there before.

"Tucker," she whispers.

"It's okay, Julia," I whisper back to her as I caress her cold cheek. "Just rest for now."

She shakes her head weakly. "I want to tell you. Right before I landed in the water. I—"

"Is she okay?" Cynthia shouts, sounding panicked.

The boat is right behind us, and my sister is standing on the edge of it looking like she's about to have an anxiety attack.

"She's fine," I tell her. "Just a little waterlogged."

Julia's eyes are closed, and she's breathing heavily when I turn back to her. The poor girl looks exhausted. "Your ride is here," I whisper to her. "You can tell me that you love me later."

Her eyes stay closed, but her lips curl up into a soft smile.

I carefully slide my arms under her and pick her up. She curls her arm around my neck and smiles as she looks at me. My heart is racing harder than when I dove off the cliff. I've always wanted to have Julia in my arms, and now that I do, it's better than I ever imagined.

I wait until the boat lines up to the rock and then I carry her onto it, holding her close to my chest, and close to my heart.

~

I can still feel her in my arms when I walk into the resort. I've been savoring it the whole bus ride home. I sat by myself in the back, closed my eyes, and pictured everything about that moment: her cold wet skin against mine, her hair tickling my arms, the look of her gorgeous green eyes gazing up at me, the intense feeling like it was only the two of us in the whole world.

I try to think of a better moment in my life, but I'm coming up short.

She's back to her regular self as she walks into the lobby, joking around with my sister and her other friends. I steal quick glances at her every few seconds, wishing that it was just the two of us once again.

Whatever moment we had is over, and it appears like she's gone back to hating me. She hasn't said a word to me since I carried her onto the boat.

With a sigh, I turn and head back to my room. A minute later I hear footsteps racing up behind me.

"Tucker." It's her.

I take a deep breath, preparing myself to turn around. Every time I see her, it feels like someone has their hand wrapped around my heart and is squeezing it.

She's standing there, looking shy as she bites her bottom lip. "Tucker. I just want to say thank you. For saving my life."

I smile at her, playing it off like it was nothing. "I was just trying to get some mouth-to-mouth action."

The tension releases from her face and she laughs. "I'm sorry I puked on you instead."

I smile at her. "Think nothing of it."

She takes a deep breath and lifts her shoulders, looking like she's ready to leave. "Well, if there's anything I can do to repay you, like saving *your* life sometime, let me know."

She gives me one last smile, turns, and walks away.

My heart is pounding as I watch her. "Wait," I call out to her. "There is."

She turns with a skeptical look on her face. "There is?"

I grin. "I want a date."

"A what?"

"I want to take you out for dinner."

She shakes her head. Violently. "No way."

"I saved your life."

"Take me back to the cliffs and drown me."

She makes me laugh. "You said *anything*."

"Not that," she says, crossing her arms over her chest.

I raise my chin as we stare each other down. "That's what I want. I saved your life. I want a date."

"Oh, God," she mutters as she rubs her forehead. "It's like being indebted to Tony Soprano."

"A Tony Soprano with abs."

She shakes her head as she looks up at me with disbelief. "Only you would exploit saving a girl's life to then guilt her into accepting a date."

I just stare back at her with a serious face. "I've always wanted to go on a date with you, Julia. I'll take it any way I can."

"Fine, Mr. Unromantic," she says, grinning. "You've guilted me into it. Tomorrow night." She lets out a long sigh as her eyes drop down to the tiled floor. "I can't believe I'm doing this."

I give her a smirk. "Wear your sexiest underwear."

Her eyes narrow on me. "I won't."

"That's fine with me," I answer with a grin. "No underwear works even better for me."

"Mphm," she grunts in frustration before turning and charging away.

It takes everything I have not to do a little touchdown dance. *I have a date with Julia! Fuck yeah!*

My eyes never leave her as she walks back through the lobby and then leaves with Tanya, disappearing into the other side of the resort.

My heart is drumming in my chest as it finally hits me. I'm taking Julia out *tomorrow*. Thoughts start racing through my head. This date has to be perfect. I have to blow her away.

I definitely have a lot of planning to do.

The warmth radiating through my body turns to cold chills when I see the last person I want or expect to see come stepping off a bus and strutting into the resort like she owns the place.

Fuck!

It's my ex. Stacy.

What the hell is she doing here?

The blood is draining from my face as I charge right up to her. "Stacy," I hiss. "Why the hell did you come here?"

"Hi, honey," she says, smiling as she throws her arms up to give me a hug. I plant my palm on her chest and push her away. She flicks her blond hair behind her shoulder as her fake smile turns into an icy glare.

Stacy can turn from sweet little girl to raging super bitch in the blink of an eye. It's because the sweet little girl bit is only an act. The raging super bitch is the real her and is always brewing close to the surface.

"Why are you here?" I snap at her again.

She rolls her eyes. "You invited me." She holds her hand out with an annoyed look on her face. "Give me a key card to our room. I want to freshen up."

I stare at her outstretched hand in disbelief. She's even crazier than I thought.

"Have you lost your mind? We broke up. That means I don't want to see you again. *Ever*."

She shakes her head, sending her blonde hair bouncing from side to side. "That wasn't a breakup. That was just a fight."

I speak slowly so she'll understand every word. "That. Was. A. Breakup."

"Whatever," she says with a shrug. "I'm here now, so it's too late."

"No, it's not," I shout. I want to pick her up and throw her onto a departing bus.

"Stephanie?!?" a voice shouts out, ringing through the lobby. I turn and see my sister charging over like an angry bull. Her face is as red as the inside of a volcano, and she looks like she's about to erupt.

Stacy grins as she crosses her arms, glaring at my sister as she stomps over.

"What the *fuck* are you doing here?" Cynthia shouts as she charges up to her, stopping an inch from Stacy's nose.

"Wha—" I mutter, looking back and forth between them. Cynthia knows Stacy? How? Why is she calling her Stephanie? I'm so confused.

"Get the fuck off my resort!" my sister shouts in her face.

My ex just grins back at her. "I'm an invited guest," she says, looking like she's loving every second of this.

"Ha!" Cynthia shouts. "Who the hell invited you?"

Stacy's face lights up with pure joy. "Your *brother* did."

Cynthia's face drops as she turns to me with a look of pure betrayal. She's looking at me like I just murdered her puppy in front of her.

"Satan!" someone yells from behind me. Megan comes charging over, holding her two index fingers up in front of her like a crucifix. "Begone, Lucifer!"

"Hi, Megan," Stacy says, grinning at her.

Megan knows her too?

"What the hell is going on?" I ask when I can finally find some fucking words. "You guys all know each other?"

"Unfortunately, yes," Megan says, standing shoulder to shoulder with Cynthia. "Tucker, meet Stephanie, the lord of the underworld."

"You're dating her?" Cynthia asks, staring at me in disgust.

I shake my head. "No way. I broke up with her. I don't know why she's here."

"You invited me," Stacy says.

"Come on, Stacy," I spit out in frustration. "That was before we broke up."

"You didn't uninvite me," she says with a shrug.

"*This* was the Stacy you dated?" Cynthia asks, pointing at her. "Her real name is *Stephanie*."

I shake my head. "I'm so confused."

"Her real name is Stephanie. She's Lucas' sister and Chase and Ethan's cousin," Cynthia explains. "She's also Megan's sister-in-law."

"Not by choice," Megan adds.

"She tried to ruin Megan's and then Tanya's wedding," Cynthia continues. "She's pure evil. And I want to know what the hell she's doing here."

Stephanie's heated eyes are narrowed on my sister. "Do you really think I'm just going to let what happened slide?" she asks in a fierce tone. "Don't you know me at all?"

"Unfortunately, yes," Cynthia says, not backing down.

"What the hell did *we* do?" Megan asks.

Stephanie whips her head around to glare at her. "You four bitches ruined my wedding day!"

"We weren't even there!" Cynthia shouts.

"I was!" Megan says, raising her hand. "Best wedding ever!"

Stephanie growls at her. "You guys put the video of me looking inappropriate on YouTube!"

"You looking inappropriate like screaming like a four-year-old and trashing your own wedding until you got tossed out by security?" Cynthia asks.

Stephanie looks furious. "I wanted the *pink* roses!"

Cynthia shakes her head as she stares at her. "You're psychotic."

"No," Stephanie says, raising her chin in the air. "I'm just a modern-day woman who gets what she wants."

Megan sticks her finger in Stephanie's face. "You're a modern-day maniac who should be locked in a padded room!"

Stephanie isn't hearing any of it. "You ruined my wedding. I'm going to ruin yours."

"Your fiancée ran away from you," Cynthia says with her voice racing. "You trashed the reception, and security threw you out! How is any of that *our* fault?"

"I was in jail because of you," Stephanie says.

"You were in jail because you smacked a cop," Cynthia shouts back.

"Wait," I say, trying to keep up. "What happened?"

Cynthia steps toward her, and Stacy, or Stephanie, or whatever her name is, holds her ground. "So, you're telling me you tracked down my brother, changed your name, and seduced him just so you could come to my wedding and try to ruin it?"

Stephanie nods proudly. "Yes."

Megan looks stunned. "You're a super-villain," she whispers.

I'm still not sure I know what's going on, but I do know that I don't want her here, Megan doesn't want her here, and Cynthia sure as hell doesn't want her here, so it's time for her to leave.

"All right," I say, grabbing her arm. "You're not staying with me, so get back on the bus, and go back to whatever hole you crawled out of."

Stephanie looks down at my hand wrapped around her arm and starts screaming like the drama queen that she is. "Stop! Stop!" she screams as tears start welling in her eyes. I'm not even holding her hard at all. "He's assaulting me! Help!"

The owner comes rushing over as I let her go. There aren't even marks from my fingertips. I was barely touching her.

"Is there a problem here, Miss Cynthia?" the owner asks.

"Yes, Lars," Cynthia says, pointing to Stephanie. "She came here uninvited with the intention of ruining my wedding. She doesn't have a reservation, and she's trespassing on your resort. Can you please remove her immediately?"

Lars turns to Stephanie. "Do you have a reservation, Miss?"

Stephanie shakes her head. "I would like to book a room."

Lars sighs. "Unfortunately, we're full to maximum capacity. You'll have to stay someplace else."

"Ah, that's too bad," Megan says sarcastically.

"Come with me," Lars says, waving Stephanie over. "I'll help you find another hotel or maybe a flight back home if we can't find anything."

She grits her teeth as she glares at Megan and then Cynthia. She exhales long and hard, raises her chin in the air, and then goes with Lars without saying another word.

"That was... interesting," I say as we watch her walk into Lars' office. "At least she's gone."

"She's not gone," Megan says, shaking her head. "That chick is like a cockroach. You can't get rid of her."

Cynthia sighs, looking like she's going to cry. I give her a hug and her body crumples in my arms.

"She's going to ruin my wedding."

I grab her shoulders and hold her body out, staring into her eyes. "She won't. I won't let her. I promise."

Cynthia doesn't look so sure. "You don't know that girl. She's pure evil."

"I'm your big brother," I say with a fierceness that surprises me. "I'll take care of it."

Cynthia exhales long and hard before she nods. "Okay. Thanks, Tucker."

I gulp as I look back at Stephanie through the glass walls of Lars' office. She's sitting in front of his desk and flipping her hair back.

I knew she was crazy, but I didn't think she was legitimately, certifiably crazy. I just hope I can keep my promise and keep her away from the wedding.

My little sister is counting on me.

CHAPTER SEVEN

DAY TWO

Julia

"Can you believe it?" Cynthia asks, still looking like she's in shock.

"With that bitch, I can," I say, shaking my head. We're just finishing up dinner, and Cynthia is still talking about Stephanie showing up.

"She's gone now," Chase says, placing a hand on my best friend's shoulder to try and calm her down. "You don't have to worry about her anymore. She's not staying with Tucker, and there are no rooms left on the resort. Lars said so himself."

Cynthia sighs. "Have you ever met Stephanie?"

Chase cringes. "You're right. She'll be back." He looks down the long table to where his buddies are talking. "Look. I have a whole team of Navy SEALs I can mobilize."

"It's not enough," Megan says, shaking her head.

"A team of Navy SEALs was enough to find and take out Osama bin Laden. We can handle a cunty spoiled brat."

"I think you're underestimating her," Megan says. "She makes Osama bin Laden look like a girl scout selling stale cookies."

For once, I think Megan may be right. Our group has had three destination weddings, and Stephanie has shown up to all three of them. She was invited to one.

This girl has a black belt in attention whoring, and we all hate her. When she's not handing out backhanded compliments or passive aggressive comments, she's stealing wedding dresses and stealing boyfriends. She has no shame.

As shocked as I am that she showed up, I'm even more shocked that Tucker had dated her. He has some explaining to do on that one.

"Who wants to go to the Casino tonight?" Chase asks the table. His Navy SEAL buddies start cheering. "I'm in the mood to make some money!"

Cynthia is sitting on my left. She leans close to me while her fiancée is distracted. "Can you keep an eye out for her?" she whispers. "We both know she's not going to give up this easily."

"Definitely," I say, nodding. "I take my maid of honor duties seriously."

I glance down the table to where Tucker is sitting beside his mother. She has her iPad out and is showing him something that he seems totally disinterested in. It's probably a news article debating that the earth is flat or something equally ridiculous.

I can't believe that he dated Stephanie. I can't believe that I have a date with him.

He's taking me out tomorrow, and the worst part is, I'm excited for it. I should be planning excuses or escape routes, but instead, I'm planning what I'm going to wear and how I'm going to do my hair. *Ugh.* I make myself sick.

Tucker's honey-colored eyes dart over to mine, and I quickly drop my eyes to my lap as my cheeks get hot. When I look up a few seconds later, he's still watching me.

Tanya is sitting beside me on my right. She's grinning as she watches us. "So, you and Tucker?" she whispers with a knowing grin. "What happened on those rocks?"

"What are you talking about?" I ask, playing dumb.

"When he pulled you out of the water," she whispers. "Were you lying there out of breath while he held you in his muscular arms and then he leaned down and touched his lips to yours, giving you mouth-to-mouth resuscitation?"

"No," I say, taking a big gulp of wine. "I threw up all over myself."

She laughs. "Some guys are into that, I guess."

I giggle along with her. "He's taking me out on a date tomorrow," I whisper. I just have to tell someone.

"What?" she shouts, a little too loud. People at the table look at us but then continue with their conversations when we sit there silently for a while.

"How did that happen?" she asks when all of the attention is off us once again.

I tell her how he wanted to go on a date with me in exchange for saving my life. Only a selfish prick like Tucker would want to get repaid for saving someone's life.

"I think it's going to be good for you two," Tanya whispers. "Everyone can see that you two have had a thing for each other since you were kids."

I scoff. "Yeah, right. What have you been drinking? You're not supposed to consume alcohol when you're pregnant."

"It's pretty obvious," she says with a shrug. "He's not a kid anymore. Maybe you should give him a chance."

I shake my head. He's still the same asshole I've always known. "He'll get his date. Nothing more."

The group gets up, and we all head over to the resort's Casino. I keep my distance from Tucker the entire time and walk around watching everyone gamble. Tanya and Megan are playing the penny slots, but even that is too rich for my blood.

"Look at this!" Tanya says, waving me over. "I put in three dollars, and I'm up seventy-seven cents!"

She pulls the lever on the side of the penny slot machine again and gets three cherries. "Woo-hoo!" she shouts as the machine rings and her money goes up. "I'm rich!"

"How much did you win?" Megan asks.

"Forty-six cents!"

Megan nods her head. "Nice!"

"I think I'm going to quit while I'm ahead," Tanya says, biting her lip nervously. She's only up a dollar and twenty-three cents.

"Good idea," Megan says. "Because you have to know when to hold them."

"Oh, no," I mutter. "You're not allowed singing in a Casino. There's rules against that."

They just ignore me. Singing rules don't apply to these two.

They keep singing, taking turns butchering the song:

"You never count your pennies,"

"When you're sitting at the slots,"

"They'll be time enough for counting,"

"When we hit the five-dollar jackpot."

"All right, that's enough."

"Agreed."

I hurry away before they start verse two. The constant pinging of coins hitting metal and Casino chips clanking together is starting to get me anxious. It keeps reminding me of my mountain of debt that I'll never be able to repay.

Maybe I can rob a Casino. That would solve my problems.

I glance over to where the boys are playing a game of poker. There's a huge pot in the middle, and it looks pretty heated.

"What's going on?" I ask Cynthia when I walk over. She's biting her nails as she watches the game.

"There's about a grand in the pot," she says nervously. "It's only Chase, Ethan, and Tucker left in the hand."

Ethan sighs and throws his cards in the middle. "I'm out," he says, shaking his head as he gets up from the table.

It's Chase's turn to bet. He rubs his chin as he stares down his opponent. Tucker is glaring back at him.

I get shivers as I watch them. This doesn't look like it's going to end well. I slowly walk over to Tucker and stand behind him. I want to be nice and close to tell him to calm down if things get any more heated.

"Five hundred dollars," Chase says. He throws all of his chips in the middle and then pulls out his wallet. He tosses a few bills on the pile and glares at his soon-to-be brother-in-law.

"There's a twenty-dollar limit on bets," one of the Navy SEALs at the table says.

"It's fine," Tucker says curtly. He reaches into his wallet and pulls out a wad of bills. "Five hundred," he says, tossing the money onto the pile, "and I raise you another five hundred."

The table is silent except for the clinking of poker chips as the two guys face off. They're staring each other down, like more than just money is on the line. Their manhood is on the line too.

Boys are so stupid.

"I'll see your five hundred," Chase says, looking nervous. "And raise you another five hundred." He doesn't have enough in his wallet. "I'm good for it."

"Okay," Tucker says, taking a deep breath. "I'll call."

He counts out five crisp one hundred dollar bills and adds it to the pot. I stare at the money with hungry eyes. But who am I kidding? That money won't even put a knick in my debt.

"What do you have?" Tucker asks.

Chase grins as he places his two cards on the table. With the five cards showing in the middle, he has three kings. "Trip kings," he says.

Tucker sighs as he looks at his cards one more time. I'm over his shoulder and see that he has pocket aces. One of the five cards on the table is an ace. He has Chase beat.

"You got me," he says, tossing his cards face down on the table.

Cynthia cheers as Chase jumps up and hugs her. Tucker is trying to look upset, but I see the tip of his lip curling up into a smile.

"I lost enough money for one night," he says, getting up from the table. "Thanks for the game, boys."

He shakes each one of their hands and saves Chase for last.

"You'll get me back next time," Chase says as he shakes his hand.

Tucker nods. "Congratulations."

He wanders over to the bar, gets a drink, and then walks out of the Casino. I bite my bottom lip as I watch him, and before I can stop myself, I'm running out the door to follow him.

It's a gorgeous Caribbean night with a nice cool breeze

on the spectacular resort. People are walking around with smiles on their faces and sunburns on their shoulders.

I spot Tucker walking by the lit-up fountain looking hot as the Caribbean sun in his white pants and gray collared shirt.

"Tucker," I call out as I jog to catch up with him. He turns and smiles when he spots me. His sexy smile makes my legs weak, and I nearly fall to the ground.

I stop in front of him and take a deep breath. The beautiful fountain is spraying up water beside us as he looks down at me with his sparkling eyes.

"That was really nice what you did back there," I say as I curl a loose strand of hair behind my ear.

"You saw my cards?"

"I did. That was really nice."

He shrugs. "I don't want to take my sister's money. She's so proud with money, it's the only way I can help her out."

"I hear that you've done well for yourself."

He smiles. "I just have fun. I've always been competitive, and real estate investing is the perfect career to be in if you're competitive."

I smile shyly, not knowing what to say. We've always been so good at yelling and arguing with each other, but this new way of interacting—talking like civilized people—is still new to us. We haven't gotten it down pat yet.

Ethan is walking over with Tanya. She looks tired but happy as she rests her head on his shoulder.

"We're going to bed," Tanya says as they stop in front of us. "I can barely make it past ten o'clock these days."

I thread my hands through her hair and smile at her. "It will all be worth it when you're holding cute little Rocko."

"We're not naming him Rocko," she says, looking up at Ethan before he can make a comment.

"We'll talk," Ethan says.

"We have talked," Tanya answers quickly. "The discussion is over."

"We'll see," Ethan says with a smile.

Tanya just shakes her head.

I take in a sharp intake of air when I see someone walking through the resort. I didn't completely believe that she was here, but she is. I had to see it with my own eyes.

Stephanie.

She's grinning in triumph as she struts over in the world's tightest and shortest dress. "Hi, cousin," she says to Ethan. "Hi, *Yawn*-ya." She looks down at her big belly and grins. "I see that you finally lost some weight."

Tanya looks her up and down. "I see that you finally got out of jail."

"I did."

"How was it?"

"Smelly. Dirty. Full of cunts."

I grin. "Sounds like you fit in just perfectly."

She narrows her eyes on me, and it makes me gulp. A jail in Belize would bring most people to their knees, but Stephanie probably did fit in perfectly. I wouldn't be surprised if she was running the place after a few days.

"What are you doing here, Stephanie?" Ethan says, looking annoyed. "It's not enough that your life is miserable? You have to make everyone else's life miserable too?"

Stephanie grins as she looks at me then Tanya. "Just these four bitches."

Tucker steps in front of me, blocking me from Stephanie's hateful glare. "You're not staying with me, Stephanie, so you might as well just go."

She grins as she holds up her wrist, showing off her pink

bracelet that the resort gives to their guests when they arrive. "I'm here with someone else."

"Who?" Ethan asks.

She smirks as she walks away. "I'll see you guys at the beach."

We all watch her as she walks through the lobby and knocks on the owner's office. Lars steps out of his office, and my stomach drops when she kisses him on the cheek.

"Oh, shit," I mutter as he grabs her ass. She's smirking at us as they walk to the bar and disappear inside.

"I'm too tired to deal with this," Tanya says with a sigh. She and Ethan say goodnight, and they leave, walking hand and hand back to their room.

I'm still in shock at seeing the devil herself. "I can't believe you dated her," I say to Tucker.

"I can't believe I dated her either." He looks shell shocked as he stares at the bar. "She wasn't like that when we dated."

I scrunch my nose up in disgust as I look at him. "You're tainted now. I've lost what tiny ounce of respect I had for you."

"Too bad," he says, as we start walking. "We're still going on a date tomorrow."

We step onto the dark path and head back to our rooms, walking together. Our shadows are touching as we walk side by side. They look so natural together that I'm a little jealous.

"If it makes even a small difference," he says as we walk by the lit-up pool. "We didn't have sex."

I have to hide my smile. I shouldn't care, but I do. I'm glad they didn't have sex. I don't think I could be friends, or anything else, with someone who had sex with *her*.

"Goodnight," I say as I walk to my door.

He smiles at me as he walks to his. "Remember," he says with a grin. "Just knock on the wall, and I'll be right over."

"Don't hold your breath."

He grins. "One knock and I'll be right over, ready to fulfill your wildest dreams."

"On second thought, hold your breath. Hold your breath *all* night."

He's laughing as I open the door and hurry inside before I change my mind.

I can't stop thinking of him as I get ready for bed. When I'm lying there in between the soft sheets, my hand slides down between my legs as I remember his arms around me as he pulled me out of the water.

I'm already so wet, and my fingers glide through my folds easily as I replay the moment in my head. This time when I'm lying on the rocks, I don't puke all over myself. I'm looking hot as he leans down and kisses me.

"Oh, fuck," I groan as I start rubbing my clit in tight little circles. I yank off the rest of my clothes as my nipples harden and warmth floods through me.

He's right there. Right behind the wall.

I slide a finger inside my silky hole as I picture him lying only two feet away on his bed. I imagine Tucker hearing me and knowing what I'm doing. I picture him pulling out his big thick cock and stroking it as I touch myself.

The thought makes me crazy, and my back starts arching as I push my fingers in knuckle deep, picturing his shredded abs and broad shoulders.

I'm breathing heavy as I get closer and closer. I want to feel him on top of me. I want to feel his lips on my skin. I want to feel him slide inside of me, stretching me, filling me.

Without thinking, I slam my fist onto the wall and knock for him to come and make my dreams come true.

But as soon as it happens, the fantasy is gone and panic takes its place.

"Oh, shit," I mutter as I jump out of bed and grab my clothes. My pussy is so wet, my nipples so hard. I'm breathing like I just ran a damn marathon as I count down in my head.

I get to seven when there's a knock on the door.

I quickly throw my clothes on and look into the peephole. *Shit. He even looks hot when his face is all distorted through a peephole.*

"Go away!" I shout through the door.

He grins. "Let me in. You won't regret it."

"I tripped and fell into the wall," I lie. "It was an accident."

I close my eyes and shake my head. *I fell into the wall? Could I have picked a more unbelievable excuse?*

"You rang for a booty call," he says. "I'm answering."

"Well, I'm hanging up now," I shout back. My cheeks are so hot that they feel like they're on fire. "Go away!"

He takes a deep breath and sighs. "I'm right next door if you change your mind."

"I won't," I shout as he leaves.

I head to the shower, put the water on freezing cold, and step in.

Just to make sure that doesn't happen again.

CHAPTER EIGHT

DAY THREE

Julia

"What is that baby doing to you?" I ask Tanya as she sits down at the breakfast table with a leaning tower of pancakes on her plate.

Megan and Cynthia are staring at her in shock.

"I've never seen you eat pancakes before," Megan says.

"Me neither," Cynthia says, shaking her head. "What happened to your usual banana, apple, and yogurt?"

"Am I that predictable?" Tanya asks as she picks up her knife and fork.

"With breakfast you are," I say as she starts sawing through the mountain of pancakes in front of her. Tanya has eaten the same breakfast every day since we've known her, which is forever.

"I'm preggers," she says before stuffing a huge mouthful of maple syrup and chocolate-covered pancakes into her mouth.

My beach bag starts vibrating at my feet, and it makes

me lose my appetite. I take a deep breath and pull out my iPhone to see who's calling.

Crap.

"Who's that?" Megan asks. "Is there an emergency meeting down at the elementary school? Did little Sally glue her hair to the wall?"

"I wish," I say with a sigh. I stuff my ringing phone back into my bag and drop it back down to my feet. "It's even worse."

"You're not going to answer it?" Cynthia asks. "Who is it?"

"Probably Mr. Mastercard wondering where his money is at," I say, feeling sick to my stomach.

Megan shakes her head. "I told you that was a credit card and not a magical piece of plastic that makes expensive stuff appear out of nowhere."

"Megan," I say, staring at her, "for once in my life, I wish I had listened to you."

"Is everything okay?" Cynthia asks, looking worried.

I just shake my head as I fight back tears.

Tanya leans in with syrup dripping from her chin. "How bad?"

"Bad," I say with a sigh. "Guys, I'm so screwed."

I dug myself into a hole of debt and stupidity that I can't possibly get out of. Now I'm standing at the deep bottom trying to look up, but I'm so far down that I can't even see the surface.

"I bought a pair of Courrèges sunglasses last year that cost seven hundred dollars, and I only wore them once."

Megan scrunches her nose up. "Ugh. I hated those glasses. They made your face look like a praying mantis."

"I spent over thirty thousand dollars on shoes," I say, staring at them in disbelief. "I teach a kindergarten class. I could have worn slippers every day and nobody would have noticed. In January, I spent four hundred and sixty dollars on a pair of ski goggles, and I haven't skied since I was twelve. Four hundred and sixty dollars!"

"They're going to cost more like eight hundred dollars when you factor in the high interest," Megan not-so-help-fully points out.

Cynthia isn't laughing at me. She looks concerned. "What are you going to do? You have to fix this."

I lean back in my chair and sigh. My stomach is a block of nerves as I push the food around on my plate with my fork. "I'll have to get a job waitressing during the week nights," I say, contemplating my options. "I can bartend on the weekends, and I'll have to work at a camp during the summers. If I do all of that, and not spend a dime, then I can probably pay everything off in five years."

Five years! I'm going to be sick.

"That's not so bad," Tanya says. She always tries to stay positive. But there's *nothing* positive about this. My life will be nothing but work for five years. Nothing but work, and I'll have to quit my favorite pastime: shopping.

There's another thing too. "But I'm single," I say, slumping even further down in my seat. "There goes any chance I have at finding and keeping a boyfriend, let alone getting married."

"You should try to win the lottery," Megan says, mocking me.

I drop my head onto the table, and it lands with a thump. It's the closest thing I can find right now to burying my head in the sand, so I keep my forehead pressed against the table for a minute. I'll come up when I feel better. Hope-fully it will be sometime before dinner.

Just when I think things can't get worse, they do.

"Are you eating like a dog now, Julia?" It's Stephanie's voice. "Good for you. It's about time you embraced your inner bitch."

I raise my head and glare at the unwelcome blonde standing at our table. My eyes are narrowed on her, trying my best to intimidate her, but the napkin sticking to my forehead is kind of ruining the effect.

"You want to meet my inner bitch, Stephanie?" I ask in a tight voice. "Keep standing right there."

She raises her nose in the air, looking indignant. "When you're dating the owner of the resort, you can stand wherever you want."

Cynthia turns pale when she spots the owner, Lars, walking in. He walks up to Stephanie and kisses her on the cheek.

"Good morning, ladies," he says to us with a nod. "Enjoying your breakfast?"

"We were," I say, glaring at Stephanie.

"Good," he says with a smile. He turns to Stephanie and slides his hand around her lower back. "I'll be sitting over there when you're done catching up with your friends."

"Okay, lover," she says before giving him a deep kiss on the mouth.

"Ew," Megan says, gagging as they tongue wrestle in front of us.

Lars looks dizzy when they finally pull away. He stumbles over to his table with red cheeks.

"Classy," Tanya says as she stuffs a huge forkful of pancakes into her mouth.

Stephanie is looking pretty satisfied with herself as she grins at us. "Well, I have to go to my date. He's already in love with me. I made sure that he had the night of his life last night."

"You better ride it while you can," I say, grinning back at her. "It's only a matter of time before he finds out you gave him chlamydia."

"And gonorrhea," Tanya adds.

"And that he unwillingly impregnated you with the Antichrist," Megan says.

The four of us burst out laughing, which makes Stephanie even angrier.

"Ha. Ha. Ha," she says in a flat voice. "We'll see who has the last laugh at the end of the week."

With a flick of her hair, she struts over to Lars' table, sits on his lap, and continues their disgusting make out session.

"How can anyone kiss her?" Cynthia asks, staring at them in fascination. "Wouldn't her saliva burn like acid?"

"I'm already queasy from the pregnancy," Tanya says, looking away. "I don't need to see this."

"You're queasy from eating a dozen pancakes," Megan corrects.

"You're right," Tanya says, grimacing as she looks down at her plate. "I better switch to waffles."

"That bitch is going to pull something," Cynthia says, watching them. "This is all making me very nervous."

I cringe as I watch Stephanie sitting on Lars' lap with her tongue down his throat. I start to wonder if she's ever done that with Tucker, and I immediately start getting jealous.

These feelings are so confusing to me. I hate Tucker, so I should be happy if he dated someone as evil as Stephanie, but the thought of them together just makes me want to puke.

My phone rings again, and my body twitches in response.

What a morning. I glance over at the bar by the pool and

wonder if it's open yet. I could use a few dozen drinks. Or better yet, I can hand them a job application.

We've been lounging around the beach all day, sipping cocktails, and working on our tans. I still haven't seen Tucker once. Maybe my luck has finally turned around and he fell into the fountain and drowned.

"Where's your brother?" I ask Cynthia who's lying next to me, soaking up the sun's rays with a strawberry daiquiri in her hand.

She raises her sunglasses onto her head and shrugs. "He said he had something very important to do on the island today, but he wouldn't tell me what it was."

I'm wondering if it has anything to do with our date when I catch myself about to smile. I bite my bottom lip to stop that from happening. People don't normally smile when they're forced to go on a date with their nemesis.

"Hmm," I say, trying to look like I'm not dying to know what it is. "He didn't say anything?"

Cynthia shrugs. "He's probably looking around the island for work. Trying to find a new investment property or something. He rented a car and everything."

I take a deep breath as I turn back to the ocean, watching a pelican skid across the sparkling turquoise water as he lands.

My heart starts pounding when I think of the embarrassment of last night. I wonder if he knew what I was doing when I knocked on the wall.

No. He definitely believed me. People walk into walls all the time. Especially while they're sleeping.

Ugh.

My cheeks start to heat up as my chest tightens. He definitely knew.

"What should we do tonight?" Cynthia asks as she stares out at the gorgeous ocean in front of us. "We can get everyone to go dancing or go to the Casino again. Or maybe we can all grab some beers from our mini fridges and hang out on the beach."

"Uhm," I say, feeling my stomach roll. "I have a date."

Cynthia jerks up into a sitting position so fast that she spills her drink on her stomach. "A date?" she asks with her jaw hanging open. "With *who*?"

I swallow hard, keeping my eyes forward and not on my best friend's shocked face. "Uhm... with your brother."

"WHAT?!?"

My eyes dart around at all of the people looking at us. I smile nervously at them.

"With my *brother*?"

"Yup," I mutter under my breath.

She gets up and sits on my beach chair. I swallow hard as she takes off my Garrett Leight sunglasses and stares into my eyes. "Explain."

I tell her how he guilted me into saying yes for a date after saving my life.

"So, you're going out?" she asks, still looking unsure. "On a date? With my brother? Tonight?"

"Yes, yes, yes, and yes," I say, feeling uncomfortable under her intense stare.

I'm actually going on a date tonight with Tucker. God those words sound all wrong when they're put together.

Cynthia sits back in her chair and wipes the strawberry daiquiri off her stomach when the crazy thought finally sinks in. "I always thought you two would either marry each other or murder each other. I'm glad it's the former."

"We're not married yet," I say with a sigh. "Murder is still a very viable option."

Cynthia grins as she slides her sunglasses back down over her eyes. "If you're going to murder each other, please wait until *after* the wedding."

I smile as I slip my sunglasses back on. "You got it."

Although I might be singing a different tune tonight.

CHAPTER NINE

Tucker

I've been nervous all day. It's not like me to get nervous, but I'm finally about to get something that I've always wanted, and an opportunity as good as this will make even the cockiest and most confident of men get nervous.

I take a deep breath as I look myself over in the mirror one last time. My hair is slicked to the side, I'm wearing the button-up shirt that always gets looks from the ladies, and I'm wearing my lucky underwear. I'm as ready as I'll ever be.

My heart starts thumping in my chest as I turn off the lights and head for the door. Tonight is going to be perfect. Julia won't know what hit her.

I spent the day driving around the island, getting everything ready for the best first date in the history of first dates. First, I booked us a luxurious staffed catamaran all to ourselves. We'll be dining on expensive champagne and fresh seafood hors d'oeuvres as the Captain sails us out to sea while the sun sets in front of us. I can already see it perfectly. Julia's silky black hair will be flowing in the wind as I make her smile and laugh. She'll see a new side of me that she's never seen before, and we'll get along great.

Next, the catamaran will sail up to a secluded and uninhabited island that I heard is spectacular. There's a gorgeous white sand beach in front of thick lush rainforest. There will be a beautiful table for two set up next to a roaring fire. Julia will be thrilled and awed as we walk barefoot through the cold sand up to the table where three waiters in tuxedos will be waiting to serve us. We'll have a 1998 Leeuwin Estate Chardonnay waiting in a bucket of ice. We'll sip on the wine and enjoy each other's company as the chef lights up the barbecue on the beach and starts grilling the fresh marlin and preparing the live lobsters that I ordered. We'll slowly fall in love as the violinist I hired begins playing softly to us as the stars come out overhead. Julia's beautiful face will be lit up by the candles, and her smile will take my breath away as I gaze into her eyes.

Once we're done with our delicious dinner, we'll have chocolate truffles that I flew in from Colombia, and to wash it down, we'll have another bottle of champagne. We'll probably walk over to the water with the champagne and sit on the sand, drinking it straight from the bottle as we talk and talk and talk. Once Julia starts getting sleepy, I'll have the catamaran pick us up, and she'll fall asleep on my shoulder as we sail back to the main island.

When we arrive back, she'll be refreshed from her short nap and will want to continue this amazing date. We'll head to Kanamana, the best beach bar on the island. I reserved a table for us, so we'll continue with drinks and conversation and probably some dancing in the sand.

I grin as I step into the hallway and close the door. It's going to be perfect.

There's a lightness in my chest as I walk up to Julia's door and knock three times. Adrenaline courses through my veins when I hear her footsteps approaching on the other side. *I can't believe this is finally happening.*

My knees nearly buckle when she opens the door. She looks absolutely stunning.

Her silky hair is up, showing off the smooth curve of her neck and her sexy shoulders. I swallow hard as my eyes slowly wander up and down from her painted toenails sticking out of her sandals, up her smooth tanned legs, to her tight black dress that hugs her thighs, to her breasts that are showing just a hint of cleavage that is enough to make me want to groan out loud, and up to her gorgeous face that is looking at me shyly.

"Wow," I say as I try to catch my breath. "You're the most beautiful thing I've ever seen."

"Did you say that to Stephanie too on your first date with her?"

My shoulders slump forward as all the excitement is yanked out of me.

"Sorry," she says as her eyes drop to the floor. "I didn't mean that. I'm just nervous, and I don't know how to act around you yet. My old way just kind of comes out like an old habit."

"I get it," I say, with a nod. "Let's just be ourselves."

"That's the problem," she says with a grin. "Myself hates you. She has since you stole my purple popsicle in grade one."

I smile. "Just let me try to make it up to you. I'll buy you a thousand purple popsicles if you forgive me."

She raises her eyebrow and smiles. "I'm listening..."

We chat about the wedding and the resort as we walk to the car I rented. She's a bit stiff and looks uncomfortable, but it's not as bad as it could be. I mean, I did torture her for over a decade. It's natural for her to have her guard up.

But this night is all about seeing me in a new light. Hopefully, she'll let go of the past and we can start on our future. Together.

"Nice car," she says as I open the door for her. My eyes are all over her body as she steps in and sits down. She's so beautiful. I can't get over it.

"I should have written in the contract that we have to stay on the resort," she says with a laugh as I get in and start the car. "Where are you taking me?"

I grin at her as I throw it into drive. "It's a surprise."

She sucks in a deep breath as she takes one last look at the resort as it disappears behind us. "I'm definitely getting murdered."

Julia frowns as we pass the security guards at the gate, mumbling something about *Home Improvement*.

I pull onto the road, and she starts playing with her watch. "All right. You get *one* hour."

"One hour?!?" I ask, looking at her in disbelief. "I saved your life and all I get is *one hour?*"

"One hour," she repeats. "If you do a good job, we may be able to extend it to two."

"Wow, thanks," I say with a laugh. "Does the driving part count?"

"What do you think?" she asks me with a smirk on her lips.

"I think you're going to be begging me to keep the date going once you find out what I have planned."

She chuckles. "We'll see."

I take a deep breath, enjoying the delicious vanilla scent of her perfume as I drive. She's silent for a while as she looks out the window at the lush scenery. The resort that we're staying at is in a very secluded area of the island. There's not much around here but rainforest and more rainforest.

"And you didn't save my life by the way," she says, turning to me after a minute of silence. "I was totally capable of swimming back to the rocks."

"Oh, really?" I say with a laugh. "Is that what you think?"

She nods. "That's what I think."

"Well, I think you'd be having a date with a lobster on the bottom of the ocean right now if I hadn't rescued you."

"Too bad nobody cares what *you* think," she answers with a laugh. "I was just about to get my second wind and swim to the boat."

"Right," I say, smiling as I turn off the main road.

"Okay," she says, looking out the window at the even thicker vegetation around us. "Where are we going? Is one of your real estate investments a tiny shack in the rainforest where you murder women?"

"Yes, but unfortunately that one is in the Bahamas."

"That's a relief," she says. She leans her head back against the seat and starts to relax. After about forty minutes of driving through secluded back roads, she looks at me with a raised eyebrow. "Your hour is almost up. So far, I'm not wooed. Where are we going for real?"

I'm about to tell her when the steering wheel starts shaking under my hands and the engine starts making a loud clunking sound. "What the hell is that?" I mutter as the gas pedal stops working.

"No way we're getting stuck out here," Julia says, looking around in panic. There's nothing along this road but huge green plants with leaves the size of coffee tables and trees that stretch up to the clouds. We haven't seen another car since we turned off the main road about thirty-five minutes ago.

"It's not dead yet," I say, cursing this stupid car under my breath as it shakes and groans like a goat in labor. "We might make—" Before I can finish the thought, the car dies.

It dies a horrible, noisy, smoky death.

"So far, this date gets negative five stars," Julia says, watching with horror as white smoke pours out of the hood of the car.

I turn to her with a grin. "So, I guess this is a bad time to try and kiss you."

"You can try," she says with a straight face. "But I might bite your tongue off."

"Ouch."

"On the bright side, it might win you back a star if you're tongueless and can't talk for the rest of the night."

We sit there looking around, not knowing what to do next. "How long do you think it's going to take for a taxi to come pick us up?" she asks.

I shrug. "Let's find out. Can I borrow your phone to call?"

She looks at me with wide eyes. "It's back at the room. Tell me you have a cell phone on you."

I gulp.

"Are you kidding me?!?" she snaps, throwing her hands in the air. "We're stuck here?"

"If it makes this situation any better, I had planned to have lobster for dinner."

"We're stuck in the freaking rainforest!" she screams, looking around in panic. "Do you know what comes out of the rainforest at night?"

"No," I say, shaking my head.

"Me neither!" she shouts, erupting like a furious

volcano. "But we're fucking going to find out! It's going to be a thousand degrees in this car!"

"We'll open the windows," I say as my mind races for available options. Available options that aren't coming to me at all right now.

"Great!" she says, crossing her arms as she stares straight ahead. "We'll get eaten alive by rainforest mosquitoes. I'll look like I have chicken pox for Cynthia's wedding."

"Okay, calm down," I say, trying to bring her down a couple of notches. "It's not that bad."

"I'm stuck in the middle of nowhere with the one guy on the planet I least want to be stuck with."

Her words are like a punch in the heart. I didn't think she hated me that much.

"Fine," I say, letting my emotions get the best of me. I charge out of the car and slam the door. "Then you can stay by yourself if that will make your night better."

My blood pressure shoots up to dangerous levels as I charge down the road with my hands clenched into fists. I wanted this night to go perfectly, and I'm so frustrated that it got all fucked up before it even got started. All my planning and attention to detail is just... gone.

Maybe Julia and I weren't meant to be together. Maybe we're just too different. Like a yin and yang, but instead of completing each other, we're just meant to be kept apart for all eternity.

I glance back at the smoking car and shake my head. This is probably the universe's way of telling me that it's never going to happen, and I should stop trying.

You win universe. I'm done.

"Wait," she says, calling out to me as she steps out of the car.

I take a deep frustrated breath as I stop and wait for her to catch up.

"I can't stay there by myself," she says when she arrives.

"Are you going to be able to stand being around me?" I ask with a roll of my eyes.

"Probably not," she says with a grin, "but it's better than staying back there and being forced to go to the bathroom in the woods."

"All right," I say with a huff of breath. "Let's just start walking."

CHAPTER TEN

Julia

"My feet are killing me," I whine as we walk for what feels like two hours, but is more like twenty minutes. I wish I would have worn my running shoes instead of my Gucci sandals. For sandals that cost four hundred and fifty dollars, you'd think they'd be a little more comfortable.

"I'm starving! Where the hell does this road go to anyway?" I ask as I crush a mosquito on my arm. "I'm beginning to think it just goes around in a big circle."

"It goes to a road called Helio," Tucker says, looking frustrated. He's been walking so fast that I'm having a hard time keeping up with him.

"What's on Helio?"

"Helio street leads to Anders street, which leads to a dock."

"We were going to have dinner on a dock?"

"No," he says, looking straight ahead as he charges up

the road. "We were going to have dinner on a—you know what? It doesn't matter."

"It sounds nice." Anything other than this sounds nice. Sitting in a prison cell sounds nice compared to walking down this road in the sticky heat.

"It would have been nice," he answers. "But it doesn't matter anymore."

"Why doesn't it matter? It sounds like you put a lot of effort into it."

He looks so agitated as he runs his hand through his hair, and squeezes it into a fist. "It's just... nevermind."

"Can you slow down?" I snap. It's like he's trying to get rid of me.

He keeps walking at the same speed, maybe even a little faster.

"Hey!" I shout as I abruptly stop, planting my feet on the dirt road. "Why do you always have to be such a dick?"

He stops at once and drops his head, breathing heavily as he gives me his back. The anger seems to have left his body, but it's in mine now.

"You're the one that was a total asshole to me all through my childhood and teenage years. You're the one who insisted on this date. You're the one who rented a shitty car that blew up. And you're mad at me?!? What the hell is wrong with you? I don't even know why I'm trying to have a relationship with you, Tucker. You're as shitty as I always thought." I turn and start walking back to the car. I'd rather have mosquitoes sucking out my blood than an asshole sucking out my soul. "Just go back to staying out of my life."

My body is tense and my heart is pounding as I storm away from him, regretting ever having agreed to this date in the first place. Why did I ever think that it would end with anything but heartache, disappointment, and anger? With Tucker, those are the only three possible outcomes.

"Julia," he calls out after a few seconds. I don't turn. I don't acknowledge him. I don't care.

I can't get away fast enough. This is officially the worst date I've ever had, and that's saying a lot. Mitch Follett set a high bar when he got drunk and lit my limited-edition Carolina Herrera dress on fire, but that's a story for another time.

"Julia," he calls out, running to catch up. "Please, just stop."

I don't stop.

He circles around in front of me and faces me, walking backward so he can look at my furious face.

"I was hoping you were going to be different this time," I say as anger surges through my veins. "I was hoping you would be nice and cool and fun like you are with everyone else, but you're just the same old Mother Tucker. You told me on the hike that you were in love with me."

"I am," he says, and then shakes his head when he realized what he said. "I *was*."

"You're not," I say, stopping. He stops as I cross my arms over my pounding heart and glare at him. "This between us is not love. This is attraction gone horribly wrong. This is something that has to stop." I sigh as I stare at him. He looks so sad and disappointed. It breaks my heart, but I have to remember that all of this is *his* fault. We didn't have to be like this. This was all *his* doing.

"I think we have to face the fact that we're toxic together, Tucker. This is never going to work. We can try and be civil for Cynthia's sake, but beyond that, I don't think there's a relationship to be had."

He looks at me for a full minute before responding. "I think you're wrong."

He's so wrong that it makes me laugh. "Trust me, I'm right."

"I can make it all up to you," he says.

I throw my hands up in the air and look around with a laugh. "How are you possibly going to make it all up to me? Are you going to build me a treehouse to live in or hunt me a wild boar to eat?"

"No," he says, rubbing the back of his neck, "but I can get you to a street cart that sells soggy tacos."

I grab his shirt and yank him toward me. I'm so hungry that I'm about to start turning over rocks and eating disgusting grubs, Timon and Pumbaa style. "If you get me soggy tacos in the next ten minutes, I'll marry you and have your babies."

He grins as he drops to a knee. "I'm going to hold you to that. Hop on."

"Are you serious?" I ask.

He smiles as he looks over his shoulder, and I hate myself for smiling back. As much as I want to hate him, and as much as I want to push him out of my life for good, every time he smiles, my priorities change. Every time he smiles, I want to make him mine.

"I have ten minutes," he says with a grin. "Start your watch and hop on."

I'll try anything for food at this point. "All right Mother Tucker," I say as I set my watch and climb onto his hard, muscular back. Heat starts swirling through me as I grab his round shoulders, and he grabs a hold of my thighs with a strong grip. His palms gripping my bare skin is making me breathless.

"You have ten minutes. Starting now."

He smiles at me one last time and then starts running.

This is simultaneously the best and worst taco I've ever had. Tucker smiles as I lick my greasy fingers, looking like I'm making love to it. If there was a minister here, I'd marry it.

"Are you a minister?" I ask the kid behind the food cart.

"Huh?" he responds, looking at me with confusion in his brown eyes.

"Nevermind," I mutter before taking another glorious bite.

The tortilla is stale, the sauce is watery, and the chicken has probably been sitting in the hot Caribbean sun all day, but I can't stop eating it. I'm so hungry. I was nervous for our date and barely had anything to eat for lunch.

Tucker laughs as he hands me another napkin. "Don't accidentally eat your hand," he says as sauce runs through my fingers. "We need that finger to hold your wedding ring."

"My wedding ring?" I say with a raised eyebrow.

"You promised, remember?" he says, looking at his watch. "You said ten minutes, and I got you here in eight."

"I lied," I say, tossing the foil paper into the garbage. "I don't marry assholes."

"I'm not an asshole," he says with a grin. "I'm just a bit of a prick."

"I don't marry those either."

I take a deep breath and look around now that I have some food in me. We're in the middle of a quiet street with nothing but thick rainforest vegetation around us. It's a dirt road with hardly any traffic on it. We haven't seen one car pass since we arrived. I know this because I would have tried to hitchhike out of here if I saw one.

"Wouldn't you sell more tacos if you set up on a busy road?" I ask Johm, the twenty-something-year-old kid behind the cart. He has a nice smile, and he shows it to me as he wipes up the chopped onions on his cart.

"There's no busy roads on this side of the island," he says, with a shrug. "I get some workers from the aloe factory on their lunch break and on their way home, but not many people at this hour. I was about to close up when you two came running."

"Thanks for staying open," I say, wiping my sticky hands with another napkin. "It was delicious."

He looks proud that I enjoyed it.

"Do you live around here?" I ask him.

He nods. "At my uncle's house. We live behind his inn." His face perks up when a thought strikes him. "Do you need a place to stay for the night?"

"Does he have a car?" I ask.

"Or a bar?" Tucker says.

"Come," he says, stuffing the last of the food into his refrigerated cart. "It's just up the road. I'll show you."

"What do you think?" Tucker asks me as Johm starts pushing the street cart down the dirt road.

"I think you better start helping him push, because I don't want to sleep out here."

He flashes me those sexy teeth, rolls up his sleeves, and helps Johm push the cart. I smile as I watch him push, wishing that I was on his back again feeling those hard muscles against my clenched thighs.

A few minutes later, we arrive at the cutest little waterfront inn that I've ever seen. It would fit about two dozen guests comfortably, but it seems to be empty at the moment. The lights in the rooms are off and the beautiful tables set up outside are deserted.

"Wow," I gasp as I walk around back and look out at the ocean. There's no beach, just a large area of flat rocks that eventually sink into the calm turquoise water. Tucker helps Johm push the cart into the shed as I take off my uncomfortable sandals and explore the area. The rocks are warm and smooth under my feet, and I can't help but smile as I walk around, staring out at the gorgeous ocean. The sun is starting to set, turning the sky a subtle pink. Sailboats are drifting by in the distance, probably on their way back to the ports after a fun day at sea.

I'm so taken with the gorgeous view that I don't even hear Tucker walking up next to me.

"This place is spectacular," I whisper, enjoying it even better now that I have someone to share it with.

"I wonder why it's empty," he says, turning around.

I glance back over my shoulder at the cute little inn. Each room has a private balcony overlooking the water, with beautiful tropical flowers growing in pots. A place like this should be packed year round. It's the perfect little romantic getaway for an overworked, undersexed couple.

"Welcome, welcome," a large man calls out to us as he walks over with a huge smile on his face. He has a big bushy mustache and a big round belly. There's an equally round woman beside him with an even bigger smile.

"Welcome," he says again in a deep booming voice as he arrives, "to the Sunnyside Resort."

"It's beautiful," I say, smiling at the older couple. The air is so crisp and clean, smelling like the ocean.

"We're the owners here," the man says, waving his arm at the adorable inn. "My name is Irving and this is my wife, Yanina."

"Hello," she says with a smile that's missing a tooth. She looks up at Tucker's face and her smile gets even bigger.

"We have rooms and food available," Irving says. "We can provide you with anything you like."

"What we really need is a ride," Tucker says. He glances down at his watch and cringes. "We were supposed to be at the dock about an hour ago."

Both of their faces drop in disappointment. It seems that they haven't had any clients in a while.

"We can stay here for a bit," I say with a shrug.

Tucker turns to me with a skeptical look.

"It's so pretty," I say, turning back to the ocean. The sky is turning pinker by the second, only now there are streaks of purple and orange as well. It's the perfect place for a first date.

I gave Irving an opening and he lunges onto it like a hungry dog in the back of a meat truck. "We have fresh lobster," he says with a grin. "I just pulled them out of the water an hour ago."

"We already ate," Tucker says.

"Lobster sounds wonderful," I say, smiling up at my date.

He grins and then turns to the excited couple. "We'll take two of your biggest ones. And a couple of bottles of your finest wine."

"Excellent!" Irving says as he claps his hands.

Yanina looks thrilled as she tightens the string on her apron. "We'll make you a feast that you'll never forget."

The two of them hurry off before we can change our minds.

"You know I booked a catamaran for us," Tucker says with a sigh. "Although they probably left thinking that we weren't going to show up."

The warm breeze takes my hair along for a ride, and I tuck it behind my ear as it tickles my face. "I like it here," I say, turning back to the gorgeous view of the ocean. "And they looked so excited to have us. Do you mind?"

He smiles as he turns to face the ocean. "As long as you're happy, I'm happy."

"Lobster always makes me happy."

We stand on the smooth rocks, enjoying the spectacular sunset, not saying a word. It's strangely comfortable standing next to him, and I have to stop myself from inching toward his body.

A few minutes later, Yanina comes over with two glasses of white wine on a tray. My mouth waters at the sight.

"Thank you," I say as she hands me a glass. "Your place is beautiful. How come there aren't any guests?"

She sighs as she hands Tucker a glass. "The people want soft sand and big resorts. We have hard rocks and a small inn. Sometimes we get people, but they never come back. We don't know why."

"Well, it's beautiful," I say, smiling at her. And it really is. There are palm trees off to the sides, swaying in the wind above the colorful tropical flowers. It's a quiet place, and there are no other buildings or villas to spoil the breath-taking view.

"Enjoy it," she says with one last smile. "The lobsters will be ready soon."

"There's no hurry," Tucker says to her as she walks away.

I swallow a smile as we walk to the water and sit down on a large rock. Every few minutes, I steal a quick look at Tucker's face. The setting sun is making his honey-colored eyes look even brighter than normal. His skin is tanned and looking very kissable with a short layer of stubble coating his strong jaw.

My head is swirling with competing thoughts as I sip on the cold wine and stare out at the calm ocean. Should I give

Tucker a chance? Should I throw the wine in his face and storm out of here? Should I lunge on him and kiss him on the lips?

I have no answers.

"Do you really think we're toxic together?" he asks after a while.

I look up at him, and my heart skips when I see the sadness in his beautiful eyes. He really does seem sorry for all that he put me through.

I sigh as I turn back to the water, not knowing what to do. Do some people not deserve forgiveness? Or should everyone get a second chance?

"I think we are," I whisper after a few beats of my pounding heart. "But that doesn't mean we can't change. People change, right?"

He takes a breath of relief. "From time to time."

We look into each other's eyes, and I see hope there. Potential. Promise.

"Well, there's no time like the present," I say, raising my glass.

He smiles as he clinks his glass to mine and then takes a sip. I linger for a second, watching his sexy lips touch the glass, before taking a sip of the delicious wine myself.

I decide to give him a second chance. A *real* second chance.

But just one. If he fucks it up, I'm out for good.

"Look!" he says, perking up as he points to the ocean. I turn to where he's pointing and gasp when I see a dolphin leap out of the water.

"I've never seen dolphins in the wild before," I say, feeling my heart swell up as more and more leap out of the water, playing together.

I get goosebumps as I watch them, curving in the air

before diving back down below the ocean. Tucker shifts closer and puts his arm around me, smiling as he enjoys the show.

So maybe we were toxic. All great love stories have a rocky beginning. Right?

I inch a little closer to him, enjoying the feel of his muscular arm holding me tight.

I just hope our rocky part is over and we can get to the good stuff now.

CHAPTER ELEVEN

Tucker

This actually turned out better than I had planned. It's always more romantic when it's spontaneous and unexpected.

Irving and Yanina set us up with a candlelit table for two on the large flat rocks in front of the ocean. The wine is flowing, and the food is delicious. But the best part is the company.

Julia has had a gorgeous smile plastered on her face since we saw the dolphins. It feels good to see her enjoying herself, and she looks absolutely stunning in the candle-light, even with the plastic bib around her neck.

"I love lobster," she says as she cracks open a large claw. "But damn it's messy." She laughs as juice sprays out on her arms.

"The best dates are always a little messy," I say with a grin.

"Lobster juices are the only kind of messy you're

getting," she says, pointing a huge claw at me. We've been talking and laughing nonstop since we've sat down. She's been telling me all about her kindergarten class and all the funny things the kids say.

She tells me about one little boy who was furious at her because she told him he couldn't marry a walrus. He refused to look at her for the rest of the day.

I told her all about my time with my Uncle Jack and how he whipped me into shape. I told her about my time up in Canada and how I built my business from scratch. The conversation has been flowing great, and I can't believe that we're already almost finished dinner. The time just raced by.

I fill up her glass of wine as she starts telling me another story about one of the kids from her class. She starts cracking up halfway in, and I just stare at her in awe, wondering how I could ever have been mean to someone as amazing as her. I hate myself for it, but it's time to put all of that behind us. We're here now, and right now couldn't be more perfect.

"And then she asked me if I could marry her divorced father," she says, stopping to giggle. "I'm embarrassed to admit that I actually considered it for a second." Her slim shoulders shake as she tries to compose herself, which makes me start giggling too. Two bottles of wine will do that to you.

Her face is flushed, and her eyes are watering as she takes another sip of wine. She's perfect. I vow in that moment to never cause her any harm again. I'll spend the rest of my days showering her with love and trying to make every moment of her life better than the last.

Irving walks over with another bottle of wine. "How is the lobster?" he asks as he opens it.

"Ah-ma-zing," Julia says, shaking her head as she looks

down at the hollowed-out carcass on her plate. "I can't possibly eat another bite."

"What about drink another drop?" he asks, holding up the open bottle of wine.

She grins as she slides her empty glass over. "Keep it coming."

Irving's big belly shakes as he laughs. He fills up her glass and then offers the bottle to me.

"I shouldn't," I say with a sigh. "I have to drive back."

"We don't have a car," Julia says with a laugh. "What are you going to drive us back on? One of those dolphins?"

"Where are you and your wife staying?" Irving asks.

I'm about to correct him that we're not married *yet*, when Julia places her hand on mine, stopping me. "My husband is making me sleep in a broken-down car in the middle of the rainforest. He's not very romantic."

"We have a perfect room overlooking the ocean that has your name on it," Irving says, motioning to the sleepy inn behind him.

"What do you say, Mrs. Connor? Want to sleep in an actual bed tonight?" I ask Julia with a grin. "Let your husband make it up to you."

"We'll take *two* rooms," Julia says, smirking at me. "You still have a lot of making up to do, and I'm not that drunk."

"Not *yet*," I say, grinning at her. "We'll take two rooms," I say to Irving. "*And* two more bottles."

Julia blushes as she takes a sip of her wine, watching me with the sexiest eyes imaginable. Irving fills up my glass and clears the dirty plates from the table.

Julia finally takes off her plastic bib, which has been cruelly hiding her cleavage all throughout dinner. Now I have a hard time keeping my eyes from darting to her breasts every few seconds, but she doesn't seem to mind.

"Have you ever thought of moving back to Buffalo?" she asks, not meeting my eye as she asks the question.

I take a deep breath and watch her face as she slowly turns back to look at me. I wonder why she's asking. Is it to make conversation or because she wants to know if more nights like this lie in our future.

"I've thought about it."

"And?" she asks, leaning forward with interest.

"I would under the right circumstances. Or for the right person."

She tries to hide her smile with her wine glass but I see the tips of her lips curl up. It's the answer she wanted to hear.

"Where are you living right now?" I ask.

She turns red and looks embarrassed as she turns away. "I'm in between apartments right now," she says, looking uncomfortable. "I'm just staying with my parents until I can find something."

She stands up suddenly and grabs her wine glass. "Let's go walk around down by the water," she says, not waiting for me to respond. "I need to walk off all of this food."

A moan slides from my lips when I see the tempting curve of her ass under her sleek black dress. This is not the Julia I knew from my childhood. Her bony arms and long skinny legs have filled out into some luscious curves. My hands tingle, wanting to explore every inch of them.

I grab the half-full wine bottle along with my glass and follow her to the water. It's a full moon and it looks impossibly bright. I thought she looked stunning in the candlelight, but she looks absolutely mesmerizing in the moonlight.

Her black hair is dancing around her face as the Caribbean breeze cools us off. She looks at me and smiles shyly as the light sound of Spanish music plays from the kitchen behind us.

"Don't you love the smell of the ocean?" she asks, breathing in deep.

Normally, I love the salty smell, but right now I wish it would disappear so I could smell her delicious perfume.

We walk for a while and then sit on the smooth flat rocks, watching the dark water. "This is nice," I say, enjoying every second of it. "I didn't think it would be once our car exploded, but this is nice."

She smiles as she looks up at the stars. "I thought I would last ten minutes before throwing a drink in your face and storming out of the restaurant."

"Come on," I say with a grin. "I usually make it to twenty minutes before that happens." I glance at my watch. "I'm going on four hours, so I can't be doing that badly."

She raises her eyebrow as she looks up at me. "The night is still young."

"Then I better tell Irving that we'll skip the coffees."

She laughs. Fuck, I love that sound.

"Well, I have to agree. This is nice," she admits.

"Wait until those soggy tacos start kicking in," I say with a laugh. "Then it won't be so nice."

She smiles as she looks down at her wine glass. "The alcohol will kill any bacteria we ate."

Our eyes meet and the smiles fade away from our lips, replaced with something else. We hold each other's gaze for a long moment as something new and exciting passes between us.

It's over too soon as she turns away, taking a deep breath.

My heart is pounding as I watch the side of her face.

"So that time you ripped the streamers off my pink

bike," she says as she stares at the water. "That was because you loved me?"

"Was that too subtle of a message?"

She laughs.

"Damn," I say, shaking my head. "I should have slashed your tires too. Then you would have known how I felt."

"You had a strange way of showing your feelings, Mother Tucker," she says, stealing a glance at me.

"I must have learned it from my father," I say, feeling embarrassed once again. "But I've picked up a few lessons along the way. I'm not as hopeless anymore."

"I can see that," she says with a quick lick of her lips. "I'm excited to see what else you've learned."

I glance back at the inn. "There's a room with our name on it, *Mrs. Connor.*"

She turns a scarlet red and my heart starts thumping a little harder. "I didn't mean *that*. And besides, I reserved *two* rooms. On your card, of course."

"I was just playing. I like to see you blush."

She narrows her eyes on me playfully and then turns away with a smile on her face.

We sit there in a comfortable silence for a while, just enjoying the sound of the waves, the soft gentle breeze, and the bright stars overhead. It feels as natural and content as sitting with a lifelong friend, and I couldn't be happier. Until I am.

She shifts a little closer to me until our bodies are touching. "It's getting a little chilly," she says, even though the temperature hasn't changed.

"Are you cold?"

"A little," she says, rubbing her arms. "But I don't want to leave."

I fill up her glass with the red wine and then sit behind

her with one leg on either side of her. "Just to keep you warm," I whisper in her ear as I wrap my arms around her, keeping her close to my chest.

"Mm-hm," she hums, pretending that she doesn't like it, but she melts into my arms, resting her back against my chest.

I wonder if she can feel my heart thumping against her back.

The fruity scent of her shampoo swirls through my nostrils, and I have to focus on something else before I get hard and scare her away.

We sit like that for a long time, just enjoying the silence. We're pretty good together when we're not fighting. It's too bad we waited so long to figure that out.

Just when I'm wondering if she's fallen asleep, she shifts in my arms. "Tucker. Are you sure you've changed? Tell me this is not some evil game you're playing."

I touch the tip of her chin with my hand and gently turn her face until she's looking into my eyes. Her face is so close to mine, her perfect lips closer than they've ever been. I can feel her breath tickling my lips, making my mouth water. Her eyes are different. They're full of... I don't know. I've never seen them like this before.

"I promise," I whisper and then seal it with a kiss. Our lips touch softly at first, and I'm so overjoyed with the thought that I'm actually kissing Julia that I forget to enjoy it.

She turns in my arms and sits up on her knees so that we're face to face. Her delicate hands caress my cheeks as she pulls my face close to hers until our lips touch again. We kiss deep and passionate this time, her tongue sliding over mine, and we only pull away when our heads are spinning.

"Actually," she says as she takes my hand in hers and stands up. "I am a little cold. Let's go inside."

"All right," I say, a little bit upset that the night is going to end. I want it to last forever.

I stand up, and she pulls me toward the inn. She takes the key that Irving gave her and lets go of my hand.

"Go give your room key back to him," she says, giving me a seductive look as she walks to the inn, swaying her hips with every step. "Tell him that Mrs. Connor will be sharing a room with her husband tonight."

CHAPTER TWELVE

DAY THREE

Julia

I must be drunk.

I must be hallucinating from soggy tacos or from tainted lobster.

But I don't feel drunk. And I don't feel sick.

All I feel is excitement. All I can think of is him.

I step into the cute room and smile contently, somehow knowing that I'm making the right decision.

Every past experience should be screaming at me to stop. To abort. But I'm not thinking of the past anymore. I'm only thinking of tonight. And tonight, I want Tucker.

There's a large comfy bed in the middle of the room next to the large glass doors that open up to the balcony. There are candles lit on the night tables, giving the room a soft romantic glow. It's just what I was hoping for.

It's cozy and warm and made for lovers.

Tucker steps into the room behind me and threads his fingers through my hair. My skin explodes with shivers as he kisses the top of my head. It's such an intimate gesture, so full of love.

He's everything that I always hoped he would be but wasn't. Tucker has finally grown up into the man that I knew he was. That I always wished he was.

I turn in his muscular arms and smile at him. "Hello."

"Hello, Mrs. Connor," he says, sinking his hands into my dark hair. "I like calling you that," he says before holding the back of my head and leaning forward. I close my eyes as our lips connect in a kiss that makes my toes curl.

I fall into the kiss with every eager cell in my body, letting him consume me completely. I wrap my arms around the back of his neck, holding him right where I want him to be.

But he wants me even closer.

He leans down and grabs the back of my knees, hoisting me up into the air. I wrap my legs around him as he kisses my neck with a hunger that is a welcome surprise.

I feel his cock harden against the inside of my thigh as his lips move south, kissing my chest and then the tops of my breasts.

It should feel weird, getting kissed by my enemy like this, but it doesn't. It feels so natural, so perfect.

I reach behind my back and grab the zipper of my dress with one hand, pulling it down as he plunges his tongue into my mouth in another deep kiss.

I'm already so wet. My pussy is aching as his tongue explores my mouth. This is so fast, but right now it doesn't feel fast enough. I want him inside of me. I can't think of anything else.

I slide my hands along his muscular arms as my dress tumbles down. His whole upper body is flexed as he holds my lower back and kisses my strapless bra. My nipples are painfully hard with his mouth so close. In a desperate frenzy, I unclip my bra and yank it off.

A low growl escapes from his throat before he takes my hard nipple into his hungry mouth and starts sucking. I throw my head back and moan as his tongue swirls around me, making me pant like a dog.

"Tucker," I moan when I see the door open behind us. We were so taken with each other that we forgot to close it. "The door." I barely manage to squeak it out as he switches to my other breast, licking and kissing every inch of it.

He kicks his leg out behind him, slamming the door shut without looking back.

I shift my hips until my wet pussy is pressed up against the hard rod in his pants. We both moan when he feels my softness on his hardness. "Fuck," I groan as he presses his hard dick against my clit. My heart is pounding so hard. My nerve endings are on fire.

There are way too many clothes on our bodies.

He lowers me onto the bed, and I get a brief flash of the wooden ceiling before he climbs on top of me and drowns me in a deep kiss. I slide my hands through his silky hair, holding his lips against mine as he climbs between my open legs and presses his cock onto my throbbing pussy once more.

His kisses feel so good. Every one of them. The soft ones, the hard ones, the fast ones, the slow ones, they all feel like heaven.

"You are so sexy, Julia," he growls in my ear as he slides both hands up my thighs. My heart starts pounding furiously in my chest as his fingers glide up under my dress. He grabs my lacy underwear with both hands and grips them hard as he pulls down. "I've always wanted to do this to you. Even before I knew what this was."

I open my mouth to tell him that I've wanted it to, but only a low moan comes out as my panties slide past my knees.

If I want to stop, it's now or never. If my panties slide past my ankles there's no going back. I'll be getting fucked by Tucker.

But deep down, I know I don't want to stop. Deep down, I know that there was no going back after the moment I agreed to the date.

I want this.

I've always wanted this.

Tucker slides my wet panties over my feet and tosses them on the floor where they belong. He looks down at my spread pussy and lets out a hungry groan.

"Fuck," he moans, biting his bottom lip as he stares down with hard eyes. "You are so beautiful."

He leans back over me and kisses me harder than ever before. My breath quickens as he pulls away and stares into my eyes with a look of pure love on his face. He leans back down, kisses me softly on the lips and then stands back up.

His eyes never leave my spread legs as he unbuttons his shirt, taking his time so that he can enjoy the view.

He's not the only one enjoying the view. I drink all of Tucker in, from the intense look on his gorgeous face to the rock-hard cock jutting out against the inside of his pants.

He's so hot. My body is craving him, screaming for him, as he slides his shirt down his thick tattooed arms. His hard chest is massive, his abs heavenly. I could stare at him all night, and I plan to, once his hot seed is warming my insides.

His shirt meets my wet panties on the floor, and he flashes me a quick sexy smile before he grips each of my knees in his hands and spreads my legs further apart.

"Tucker," I moan as he bends down. I gasp when I feel his hot breath tickling my aching folds. My back arches and my toes curl, and he hasn't even touched me yet.

When he does, I nearly come on the spot. "Mmm," I moan as his silky tongue slides up from my wet tunnel to my throbbing clit. He devours me with an intensity that surprises me, but it shouldn't. Tucker has always been a little intense.

My body is on fire as his tongue settles into a steady rhythm that makes me gasp with every long lick. He pushes his tongue in deep, swirling around my wetness before moving back up and sucking my clit.

"You're going to make me come if you keep doing that, Tucker," I gasp. I sink my hands into his hair and hold him right there.

His tongue speeds up with a new determination to get me off. He reaches up with a hand and grabs my breast with a firm grip as he slides two fingers of his other hand inside me. His expert tongue and lips work my clit, and it's enough to set me off.

"Shit," I hiss through gritted teeth as my body erupts in a thunderous orgasm. My back arches, my legs shake, and my fingers grip the sheets as he steps back with a shit-eating grin on his face, admiring his handiwork.

"What are you looking at, fucker?" I ask with a playful grin as the intense waves of my orgasm finally start to dissipate. He looks pleased with himself as he slowly unbuckles his belt in front of me.

Who am I kidding? He should be pleased with himself after that.

"I'm just enjoying watching you come," he says as he slides his belt out of his pants and drops it on the floor. "It's going to be happening a lot, so you better get used to it."

"Enjoy it while you can," I say as I wiggle out of my dress. "You'll never see it again."

He laughs as he starts to unbutton his pants. My eyes are glued to the hard bulge hiding in there. I talk a big game, but my eyes and body are betraying me. I can't take my eyes off his cock.

I hold my breath as he pulls his pants and boxer briefs down in one slow movement. His long beautiful cock springs out, and I gasp at the gorgeous sight of it.

He's definitely the largest and thickest I've ever been with, and I can't wait to find out how he uses it.

My body stiffens as he climbs over me, gripping his hard shaft with a powerful grip. He slides his round tip up my folds and then pushes the thick head of his cock against my wet opening. I shiver with anticipation as he hovers over my tunnel, teasing me for a second before he slides in.

"Oh, *fuck*," I moan as he slides inside. His thick shaft stretches me wide, burning sweetly as he buries himself to the hilt inside of me. He wraps his big arms around me, and I feel so safe and protected in them.

I shouldn't feel this way with Tucker. Past experience has taught me that. But I can't help but feel that he's not the same Tucker anymore. I want to believe that he won't hurt me. I want to believe that I can give myself over to him completely.

I don't know what to believe anymore, but in this moment, I'm all his.

I cry out, loudly, as he thrusts in hard, making me feel so good that I can barely believe this is real.

He tilts my hips up, or maybe it's me, and he ramps up the pace, thrusting into me until I'm begging him to stop, begging him for more, begging him to come.

One strong hand grips my ass tightly as he slams into

me, his pelvis crushing into my throbbing clit, threatening to make me unravel again.

"You're going to ride me next," he growls into my ear as he thrusts in hard. "I want you on top of me so I can see your big tits bouncing in my face."

I can barely speak, but I manage to nod. Whatever he wants. I'll do whatever he wants as long as he keeps that big dick in me.

"All right," he says after a few more thrusts. I gasp when he pulls out of me. I reach down for his cock. It's sticky wet.

He lies on the bed and grabs me by the waist, pulling me on top of him. I guide his perfect dick back into me and start bouncing up and down on it, just like he wanted me to.

His hands and eyes are on my breasts, massaging them, kneading them, admiring them. My nipples are painfully hard under his gaze, under his touch.

His arms and chest flex, and he starts breathing heavily. "Come for me again, Julia," he growls. He starts rubbing my clit with his thumb, and I almost come instantly. His voice is tight and demanding. He'll get what he wants. "Make this tight little pussy erupt and I'll fill you with my come."

If his big dick wasn't enough, his words add to it all, and my second orgasm comes raging forward. I come even harder than the first time, and I'm falling into his arms when I hear him cry out my name and then feel him release inside of me.

His huge arms swallow me, holding me close as he nuzzles his nose into my hair. This moment is more perfect than I ever thought it could be, and I'm sad that it's going to eventually end.

"That was amazing," I whisper as I rest on his chest.

"That was long overdue," he says with a smile.

I couldn't agree more.

We lay there holding each other tight until we drift off to sleep with the cool breeze wafting in through the window cooling off our hot skin. My ear is on his chest listening to the soft rhythm of his heart. *Thump, thump. Thump, thump. Thump, thump.*

It's beating to the same beat as mine.

Thump, thump. Thump, thump. Thump, thump.

Our hearts are finally in sync.

It took almost three decades, but we got there.

"Do you think they'll cook us breakfast?" I ask as we walk out of the inn.

"I'll give them five thousand dollars for a pancake," Tucker says, rubbing his stomach. "I'm starving after that workout."

I grin as I watch him looking around. We spent the night and morning alternating between sex and sleep. My man is ravenously hungry because of me.

"I'm sure they're going to come out soon," I say, grabbing Tucker's hand and pulling him to the water. It's a gorgeous day with not one cloud in the bright blue sky. The sun is shining and the crystal clear turquoise water looks incredibly inviting.

"Look at all of the fish," I say, pointing at the colorful tropical fish swimming through the water.

"I'm going to eat one raw," Tucker says, licking his lips.

"This is such a nice place," I say, looking around at the resort. It's all big slabs of rocks rather than sand, but who needs sand with a view like this? "It would be a beautiful place for a party or for a wedding. I wonder why there's no people here."

"Uhh," Tucker says with a dropped jaw. "I think I know why."

I turn to where he's looking and gasp. Cute little Irving and Yanina are waving at us as they walk over. Completely naked.

"Oh, my God," I say, turning away quickly before the image is seared into my brain forever. Too late.

Now that it's there, I can't get it out.

"Irving and Yanina are freaks," I whisper as they walk over wearing a smile—and only a smile.

"Ah, did you two forget your bathing suits?" Tucker asks as they arrive. I have a sudden desire to admire the coconuts in the palm trees. Anything is better than staring at the coconuts on Yanina.

"No," Yanina says, shaking her head.

"This is a nudist resort," Irving says. "Did we not tell you?"

"I don't think that came up," I say, cringing. I suddenly lost my appetite. And even if I still had it, I'm definitely not eating egg whites made by a naked old man.

"We're going for a quick swim, and then we'll make you some breakfast," Yanina says as the old couple walk hand in hand into the water. Thankfully the water takes away the horrifying view.

"Now we know why it's empty," Tucker says, watching them swim away. "You have to look at Irving's saggy balls while you eat your pancakes."

"Ewww."

Tucker shrugs and then pulls off his shirt.

"What are you doing?"

"When in Rome," he says with a grin on his sexy lips. He unbuttons his pants and lets them fall down his muscular legs.

I wouldn't mind staring at that while I eat my pancakes.

"Coming?" he asks as he walks to the water as naked as a dolphin.

I take a quick look around, but there's nothing but birds and plants in sight. "Fuck it."

I quickly get undressed and run into the refreshingly cool water. I dive under and soar through the water like a superhero until Tucker grabs my ankle and yanks me back, pulling me into his naked embrace.

He smiles as I pop up, and then he kisses me softly on the lips.

Best vacation ever.

CHAPTER THIRTEEN

DAY FOUR

Julia

"Wait, who was naked?" Megan asks, scrunching her face up as I tell the girls the story.

"Irving and Yanina," I answer.

"You're telling me you spent the night with Tucker, and the only naked people were the old couple who ran the inn?" Megan says, scrunching her nose up in disappointment. "There are so many things wrong with that story. I can't even."

I laugh as I take a bite of my sandwich. We're eating lunch at one of the restaurants on the beach on the resort, and my girls are grilling me. All except Cynthia, who really doesn't want to hear about her brother's sexual exploits.

Not that I'm telling them anything. I kept the physical activities to myself.

Irving drove us back after we ate breakfast, and after some pleading, he agreed to wear shorts, but he wouldn't budge on putting a shirt on.

"So, besides the old naked couple, how was it?" Tanya asks.

"It was okay," I say with a shrug. I take a sip of my lemonade as I scan the beach, looking for him. It was definitely more than okay. I haven't been able to think about anything else since I got back.

I don't see Tucker, but I do see someone else. Stephanie is in the front of a Zumba class, bouncing around in a bikini that's *way* too tight. Her new fiancée, Lars, has a front row seat in a beach chair, watching with a creepy grin on his face.

"Look at her," Cynthia says with a look of disgust on her face. "I hope a coconut falls on her head."

The Zumba instructor swings her leg up about a foot off the ground, but Stephanie swings hers up over her head, showing the crowd of horrified families her disgusting camel toe.

"She's trying to pull something," Cynthia says, stirring her straw in her drink as she glares at her. "This is not good. She's going to fuck up my wedding."

"If she fucks up your wedding, I'm going to fuck her up," I say as I narrow my eyes on the bouncing blonde. "She's going to be begging to get thrown into a Belizean jail just to get away from me."

"It's going to be fine," Tanya says. "She tried to mess up both mine and Megan's weddings, and she didn't get anywhere. Both weddings were perfect. She's just not that smart."

"Her skull is full of cottage cheese," Megan says as she dips a pickle into her Coke. "We'll outsmart her at every turn." She puts the pickle in her mouth and bites down on it with a crunch.

"I don't know," Cynthia mutters, still watching her.

"What happened when Wendy Miller tried to break your art project in grade four?" I ask.

Cynthia locks eyes on me. "You poured purple paint in her hair."

"That's right," I say, grinning at her. "Nobody messes with my Cynthia. I'm your maid of honor, got that? This is my job. You worry about having fun on your wedding week."

"More like maid of dishonor," Megan says with a chuckle.

I slowly turn to her with heated eyes.

"Frolicking around at a nudist resort with the brother of the bride," she says with a laugh. "Not very honorable if you ask me."

"Good thing nobody asked you," I say with a playful glare.

"Tell us the real story," Megan pleads. "Julia, I need this. I've been married for too long. I miss these wild and random sexual encounters."

"Wild and random sexual encounters?" I repeat with a laugh. "You? Where did you have any of those? At your Harry Potter fanfic conferences?"

Megan looks up with stars in her eyes. "He was dressed as Malfoy. It was as magical as the foundations of Hogwarts."

"You're such a dork," I say, trying to hold in a laugh.

"Tell her what you were dressed up as," Tanya says, giggling.

"Dobby," Megan says. She continues when she sees the blank stare on my face. "The house elf."

"You had sex dressed as an elf?" I ask, shaking my head.

She shrugs. "He thought the ears were sexy."

"Anyways," Cynthia says, pushing her plate away. "Please be on the lookout for any slutty shenanigans from

Stephanie. I really want my wedding to go down without a hitch."

"Or a bitch," Megan adds.

"I'll keep my eyes peeled," I say, tossing my napkin on my plate. Just as I say it, I see Tucker walking by the pool wearing only a black bathing suit. I swallow hard as I admire his massive chest and sculpted tattooed arms. My fingers start tingling when I think back to last night (and this morning) when I got to touch them. He stops at the bar by the pool and leans on the granite to order a drink.

"I need a tall drink," I say, pushing my chair out.

Megan glances over her shoulder and sees who I'm looking at. "You need a tall drink of something, but it's not water."

"I'm thirsty," I say, locking eyes on her.

She glances down at my full glass of water on the table. "More like hungry. For some D."

"That's my brother," Cynthia says, covering her ears. "Lalalalalalalala."

"Tell us the real story," Megan begs. "I told you all about my Harry Potter elf sex."

"I really wish you hadn't," I answer.

"She's not ready to tell us," Tanya says, coming to my rescue. "That's fine. We're all just happy that you're getting along."

"She's getting along all right," Megan says with a grin. "She's getting a long D."

"I'm out of here," Cynthia says, running away before she can hear any more.

"You guys couldn't handle it," I say with a grin. I'll tell them all about it later, but right now I just have to be near him. I feel like a magnet being pulled to its other half.

"Lucky bitch," Megan says, shaking her head as she stares at me in wonder. "He's so hot."

I take two steps away before turning back to them. "A long *thick* D," I say with a wink before turning and walking away.

"Lucky bitch," I hear Megan mutter again as I leave. I giggle to myself as I leave the restaurant. I am a lucky bitch.

I fluff up my hair, put my limited-edition Valentino sunglasses on, and fix my Michael Kors bikini top as I walk over. Tucker straightens up as he sees me approaching, watching me with a grin on his face.

I'm not about to make this easy on him, so I sit on the opposite end of the empty bar, pretending like I don't know him.

The bartender hands him a beer and then hurries over to me with a wide smile on his face. "Mamacita," he says. "What are you drinking?"

"Vodka with an energy drink," I say as I slide my sunglasses on top of my head. "I was up *all night*."

"Oooooh yeah," he says, shaking his hips as he bites his bottom lip. "Doing what?"

"My taxes," I say. "It was a nightmare."

I hear Tucker chuckle from the other side of the bar as the bartender's face drops. He turns with a frown and grabs a glass and a bottle of Vodka.

I try to keep my eyes straight as Tucker makes his way over, but it's pure torture. Especially when he doesn't have a shirt on.

"Hello," he says, sticking his hand out. "Tucker Carson."

"Not interested," I say, trying to hold back a laugh. I don't even turn to look at him.

He sits down next to me anyway and sips on his beer. I

don't look at him, but that doesn't mean I don't sneak a quick peek at his thick tattooed forearm.

"Lots of girls say they're not interested in me," he says, "but in reality, they're madly in love and just don't know it. There's one girl in particular that I can think of."

"Thanks," I say to the bartender as he slides the Vodka and energy drink in front of me.

"I kept at this girl for years until she finally broke and admitted her feelings," he continues.

"Sounds like you're a stalker," I say, taking a sip of my cold drink. "Why are you harassing poor innocent girls?"

"This girl wasn't so innocent," he says, grinning as he sips on his beer. "She put out on the first date."

"She must have been drunk," I say, feeling my heart start to pound. I pretend it's from the energy drink and not from him, although it's probably the energy drink. This shit is poison.

"Maybe," he says, widening his grin. "But she put out in the morning too."

I turn to him with narrowed eyes. *Fuck he's hot.* "I wouldn't go around bragging about this poor innocent girl, who sounds absolutely stunning by the way, if you ever want her to put out again."

"Thanks for the advice," he says, looking down at me with sparkling eyes. "I'm trying to get her to put out again. Maybe after these drinks?"

I can feel my cheeks turning red as I look down at my drink that now looks way too full. "I think she might be interested in that."

I laugh as he chugs the rest of his beer like he's at a frat party. I'm not chugging vodka with an energy drink, I'll be way too wired and will be hyper enough to run a marathon.

On second thought, locked in a room with Tucker with

unlimited energy sounds like a great way to spend an afternoon, so I chug the rest of my drink.

Just as we're about to leave, Chase comes walking over. "Shit," I hear him curse under his breath when he sees Tucker at the bar. This is not good. These two have to learn how to get along. And if Tucker and I can learn how to get along, then any two people can.

"Hey, Chase," I say, sitting back down on the bar stool. "Two more days until the wedding. Are you excited?"

His face breaks out into the widest smile I've ever seen on him. "I'm counting every second."

"How many left?"

"About 183,000," he says with a laugh. "And each one is torture."

Tucker looks uncomfortable as he stands beside the bar. His body is stiff, and he's breathing heavier than he was a few of those 183,000 seconds ago.

"We're going dancing tonight," Chase says after ordering a beer. "You two coming?"

"As long as you make Megan promise not to force me to do any embarrassing synchronized dances," I say with a shake of my head.

"You know I can't promise you that," Chase says with a laugh. "Even a platoon of Navy SEALs can't stop that girl when the music starts."

"Well, I'll be there anyway," I promise. "Tucker too."

He lets out a huff of breath beside me.

Chase looks at his soon-to-be brother-in-law, and I can see his face tighten up. "Great," he mutters under his breath. "I'll see you later, Julia."

"Would it kill you to try and be nice to the guy?" I ask Tucker when he's gone. The annoyance is thick in my voice. "He's an American hero, he's a great friend, and your sister is in love with him completely. What exactly is your problem?"

"Cynthia and I have been down this road before," he says, looking agitated as he watches Chase walk back to the beach with a slight limp. "I know how this is going to play out."

"You don't know anything, Tucker," I say, starting to raise my voice. This guy is great at getting me frustrated. "You don't even know him."

"I know guys like him. They're all the same."

"No, they're not. He's not your father."

His back straightens as he turns away from me like I just slapped him.

"I'm sorry," I say, feeling like I stepped over a line that I shouldn't have. "Tucker, I..."

"I'm going for a walk." He leaves without giving me so much as another glance.

I sigh as I watch him walk under the palm trees toward the beach. This guy can go from charming to jerk in the blink of an eye.

"Who am I kidding?" I mutter to myself as I watch him go. *Maybe he is just the same old Mother Tucker.*

CHAPTER FOURTEEN

Julia

I stay with my girls throughout dinner, avoiding Tucker as best that I can. I'm still annoyed and insulted that he walked away from me after we had made plans for the afternoon. Especially since it was plans for an afternoon delight.

And all because I was trying to help him get along with Chase. He's going to be his brother-in-law whether he likes it or not, so he might as well try and make the best of it.

"*Ugh*," Megan whines. "This DJ sucks."

She's been giving the poor guy the stink eye from across the bar all night.

"We're in Aruba," Tanya says, defending the guy. "He's playing his country's music.'"

"Well, his country's music sucks donkey balls," she says, crossing her arms over her chest as she pouts. "It sounds like a raccoon is being tortured in the same room as someone learning how to play drums."

"And the Spice Girls is any better?" I ask with a laugh.

Megan looks at me with pure betrayal on her face. "Who are you?" she asks, the disgust clear in her voice.

"I'm the person who's glad that she doesn't have to dance," I say with a laugh.

"Me too," Tanya says, raising her hand.

"I'm with you," Cynthia says, sliding her heavy arm over Megan's shoulders. My best friend had a little too much wine at dinner and is feeling a little too good. "I want to fucking dance my tits off." We all laugh as she breaks out in giggles.

"You heard her, Mrs. Maid of Honor," Megan says, staring me down. "The bride wants to dance. It's your responsibility to make it happen."

"Fine," I say with a shrug of my shoulders. "I'll see if the DJ has any twenty-five-year-old music that nobody wants to listen to."

"Thank you," Megan says with a nod of her head.

I wind through the moving crowd of tourists on the dance floor to the DJ booth, keeping my head low, but he finds me anyways. He pops up in front of me like a muscular wall.

"Are you going to avoid me all night?" Tucker asks, looking hotter than ever in a tight white shirt. His face is tanned a sexy brown, and his eyes are brighter than the flashing lights over our heads.

"All week is more like it," I answer, trying to walk around him. It's not an easy task with all the bumping and grinding bodies clogging up the dance floor.

He leans down until our eyes are level. "I'm sorry. I was a jerk. Again."

"I'm used to it." I try to push around him, but a drunken dancer crashes into me, sending me flying into Tucker's big arms.

He holds me tight. I want to struggle out of his arms, but I melt into his embrace instead. "I'm worried about my sister. That's all. I saw what happened to my mother for picking the wrong guy, and I don't want the same thing to happen to her."

"He's a good guy," I say. Why can't he see that?

"I hope you're right," he says, holding me tight. "I want to make it up to you. What can I do?"

My lips curl up into an evil grin. "You can get the DJ to play Wannabe by Spice Girls."

"Done."

That was easy. I should ask for more.

"And, you can take my place in the dance routine."

I expect him to say no, but he agrees.

"Done."

"Really?" I ask, tilting my head. "But you don't know the moves."

"I know the moves," he says with a fierce determination in his eyes. "I watched every one of your rehearsals when we were younger. If I hid in the laundry room, I could watch you through the slats in the door."

"You watched us?"

"I watched *you*," he corrects. "I told you. I've always been in love with you."

He smiles down at me and my heart starts to flutter. "Go tell Megan to lace up her running shoes. It's go time."

My head is spinning as I walk back to my friends. I wasn't really sure if he was telling the truth. He was in love with me back then? He watched our practices for me?

I'll find out in a few minutes if he's telling the truth or not.

I keep my eyes locked on him as he talks with the DJ.

The DJ shakes his head until Tucker pulls out his wallet. I laugh, wondering how much this is going to cost him.

I can't help but think that watching him dance around to the Spice Girls will be worth every penny.

After the horrible local song ends and the tortured raccoon finally dies, Scary Spice rings through the speakers telling us what she really, really wants.

"Oh, shit!" Megan shouts, slamming her drink on the bar and sprinting out to the dance floor, pulling a drunken Cynthia along for the ride.

Tanya looks exhausted as she sighs and starts walking over, holding her big pregnant belly. She turns and looks at me with a shocked look. "Coming?" she asks.

I shake my head and point to the dance floor behind her. "You have a new Posh Spice."

Tanya's shoulders shake with laughter when she sees Tucker line up beside Megan and Cynthia.

I stare in amazement as he hits every move perfectly. He stares right at me as he mouths the next two lines that play through the speakers: "*If you are my future. Forget my past.*"

I laugh at that one. Megan breaks a sweat as she jumps across the dance floor with more enthusiasm than when we first performed the routine over a decade ago. Cynthia tries to keep up, but she's too drunk and crashes forehead first into her brother's stomach.

My stomach is fluttering as I watch him swing his hips to the beat. He really was hiding in that laundry room watching me. He really did have a crush on me for all those years.

I should still be upset that he was always such a prick, but it's actually kind of sweet now that I'm seeing his behavior from a different light. He was just a young kid who was in love and didn't know how to show it.

The song fades out at the end, and you can barely hear the crowd's sigh of relief over the hooting and hollering of Chase's navy SEAL friends by the bar.

"Girl Power!" Megan shouts as she throws a fist in the air, looking like a sweaty Freddie Mercury.

Tucker's eyes are locked on mine as he walks over. "Forgiven?" he asks.

"Forgiven," I say, grinning at him. "But unfortunately, I've lost what little attraction I had for you after seeing that."

He flashes his white teeth as he gives me a sexy smile. "At least I'm forgiven. Can I get you a drink?"

"I thought you'd never ask."

We head to the bar when Tucker's mother comes rushing over holding her iPad. "I got the whole thing on video!" she says proudly.

Tucker narrows his gorgeous eyes on her. "Delete it now or I'm going to acquaint it with the bottom of the ocean."

"Why?" she asks, flipping through her videos. "It's cute."

She hits play and shows us. You can hear her high-pitched laugh throughout the video.

"Can you send me a copy of that please?" I ask, giggling as I look over her shoulder.

Tucker shakes his head. "No. She can't."

"Definitely," his mother says.

"Three seconds to delete it," Tucker warns, "or the next thing to be watching it will be a starfish."

Amy clutches her iPad to her chest and runs away, disappearing into the crowd.

"Mothers shouldn't be allowed to have technology," he says, shaking his head as he watches her leave. "All they do is embarrass their kids with it."

"That video is not embarrassing," I say with a chuckle. "It's the best thing I've ever seen."

"It would have been better if you were in it."

"So, you really did watch me," I say, unable to contain my grin. "How many times?"

"*Every* time," he says. His face looks so serious. "I could watch you for hours. I still can."

I bite my bottom lip as I turn to the bar to order a drink. "You can watch me anytime you want," I say, looking over my shoulder at him. "Creeper."

The bartender makes eye contact with me and raises his eyebrows.

"Two bee-"

"Esteban," a voice beside me says, interrupting me. *Ugh.* It's Stephanie.

The bartender turns away from me and focuses on her. "Yes, Miss Stephanie. What can I get for you?"

She shoots me a triumphant sneer before ordering two martinis.

"I was about to order," I say through gritted teeth. "I was here first."

She looks back at Tucker standing behind me and grins. "I was there first, but you don't hear me being a little bitch about it."

Heat flushes through my body as I fantasize about grabbing her blonde hair and slamming her face into the sticky bar.

"Oh, please," Tucker says, rolling his eyes. "I dumped you the second you showed a flash of your true self."

"You couldn't handle my true self," Stephanie says, thrusting her chin in the air.

"Hitler couldn't handle your true self," I spit back at her.

"Enjoy my sloppy seconds," she says as the bartender places two martinis in front of her. He turns to take my order next, but Stephanie shakes her head. "Don't serve her."

The bartender looks at me with an apologetic look on his face and then moves on to the other waiting customers.

"What the hell?" I shout to him, but he doesn't turn back.

"And you four bitches are all banned from the dance floor until further notice," she says, loving every minute of this. "You're scaring my customers away with your humiliating dancing."

"*Your* customers?" I repeat with a scoff. "You own the place now?"

I can feel the evil radiating off her as she grins at me. "I own the owner. I've got him wrapped around my finger. Literally."

My stomach drops as she lifts her hand and shows me a diamond engagement ring on her ring finger. *Shit. We're screwed.*

"Enjoy your stay at my resort," she says, picking up the martinis off the bar. "While you still can."

I'm worried I'm going to puke all over my Gianvito Rossi pumps as she struts away with the two drinks. She shoots me one last victorious smirk before sitting on Lars' lap. She hands him a martini and then shoves her tongue down his throat.

Cynthia comes stumbling over, looking even drunker than before. "Hey, sexy!" she shouts in my face, showering me with her alcohol-soaked spit. "Are you having fun?"

"*You're* having fun," I say back to her, trying to force out a smile. I can't tell her now. Either it will ruin her night, or she'll be too drunk to understand me anyway.

She squeezes my arms, digging her fingertips into my

biceps. "I'm marrying a Navy SEAL," she shouts, looking ecstatic. "On the beach! I can't fucking wait!"

My chest tightens. Let's hope that she gets married on the beach. I glance over at Stephanie, who is glaring at us while Lars cops a feel over her dress.

Because Cynthia will be getting married in the parking lot if that evil cunt gets her way.

~

"It's going to be fine," Tucker says, trying to make me feel better. "We won't let her ruin the wedding."

"You don't know this girl," I say as we walk through the dark resort. The party died down after Chase brought Cynthia home when she got too drunk to stand, and everybody just kind of went their separate ways.

"I did date her, remember?" he says, shaking his head.

"I'm trying to forget that," I say, feeling sick to my stomach like I always do when I picture them together.

"Nothing happened," he says, quick to remind me. "I don't put out on first dates."

I raise an eyebrow as I look up at him. "Do I have to remind you of last night? That was a first date."

"You don't count," he says, smiling at me. "It doesn't count when it's the girl you're going to marry."

"Easy boy," I say with a laugh. "Let's get one wedding done at a time."

The resort looks gorgeous at night with the lit-up pool snaking along the walking path. It winds through the resort, lighting it up in a turquoise glow. It's quiet at night with only the sound of the soothing waves in the distance mixed with the beat of the club somewhere far behind us. I glance up at the bright stars, wondering how this is all going to play out.

Not just the wedding, but us. In three days, we'll be going our separate ways. I'll be on a plane to Buffalo, and Tucker will be on a plane back to Minnesota. Actually, I'll be on a plane to Colombia with a seven-hour layover before heading back to the states.

With all the excitement and my attention focused on Tucker, I forgot all about my debt. The stress and anxiety comes crashing down on me just thinking about it.

You're here with Tucker. Live in the moment, and try to forget about it. I tell myself. *You'll have plenty of time to stress about money when you're working four jobs.*

"What now?" I ask, trying to get my mind off my money problems.

"I don't know about you," he says, starting to unbutton his shirt. "But I could go for a swim."

I look around nervously as he takes off his shirt. "The pool is closed."

"Perfect," he says with a mischievous grin. "Then no one will see us skinny dipping."

I'm hoping that he's kidding, but he starts unbuckling his belt.

"Security is walking around," I say, looking from side to side. There's no one in sight.

"Then we'll be extra quiet," he says, sliding his pants and underwear down. I let out a groan as I see his big cock lit up by the light of the pool.

My mouth waters and my nipples harden as I stare at it. "Tucker!" I whisper as he climbs into the pool, taking the mouth-watering view of his dick away from me. "This is crazy!"

"Vacations are made for crazy," he says with a grin. He slides his wet hand through his hair, taunting me with his sexy eyes. "I'll be in there," he says, motioning to the entrance of a little grotto in the pool. It's not totally private, but it's a little bit more private than where he is now. "I'll be waiting in there with my big dick. I hope you and your tight little pussy come and join me."

I swallow hard as he dives under the water and swims away, giving me a flash of his perfectly sculpted ass.

"Shit," I whisper, starting to panic as I look around. It's late at night and there's nobody around, but I'm still shy to go skinny dipping in a public place. This morning was different with only Irving and Yanina around, and I was still hiding my Kibbles and Bits.

But I can't stop thinking of that long dick waiting for me. "Just do it," I whisper to myself, trying to psyche myself up.

I hurry behind a cluster of palm trees as my heart starts thumping nervously in my chest. I slide my Soft Joie dress down, quickly take off my bra and underwear, say a little prayer, look around one more time, and then hurry into the pool.

The water is cool and feels electric on my skin, making my nipples as hard as diamonds. I dive under the water before I chicken out and swim to where my big dick is waiting for me.

"What do we have here?" Tucker asks, grinning as I pop out of the water. "A naked mermaid?"

His back is against the wall of the pool with his arms spread out along the edges. He looks gorgeous wet, and the light of the pool is just adding to the sexy effect. I look around nervously, but there's only tropical bushes and plants around us, hiding us from anyone walking by.

He looks down at my breasts as I walk up to him. "You are fucking stunning," he says, shaking his head.

As soon as I'm within his reach, his hands are on me,

pulling me closer. I let out an involuntary moan as his thick cock brushes against my thigh.

"And you are making me break the law," I whisper back to him.

"I should have brought my handcuffs," he says, hovering his lips over mine. "To punish you properly."

His lips connect with mine, and I'm glad I'm in the water with his arms around me because my legs give out on me. The kiss is hard. Fast. Demanding. He rips the air out of my lungs as he claims my mouth.

This man drives me wild. Arousal courses through me, and despite the cold water, I can still feel the heat between my legs. He makes me crazy.

This is crazy. Fooling around naked in a public pool. It's crazy. He does this to me.

I sink my fingers into his hair and pull him toward me, wanting him even closer. I moan into his mouth when I feel his hard cock press up against my stomach.

He moans back into mine when I reach down and grip it with excited fingers.

I wasn't planning on this. I wanted a quick swim and then a quick getaway, but now all I want is for him to fuck me here and now. I don't care if the whole resort hears. I don't care if the whole resort sees. The threat of that is just heightening my arousal. It's adding to the effect.

His hand glides through the water, and I gasp as his fingers slide through my folds. He teases me by tracing the entrance to my hole and doesn't give in even when I grind my hips on his hand.

"Oye!" a voice shouts out of nowhere.

Panic seizes me as I release the cock and grab onto Tucker's large body, hiding my breasts from the flashlight pointing right at me.

My heart starts racing even harder as a heavy feeling settles into my stomach. *Shit! I'm naked!*

"Out of the pool!" the security guard shouts as he comes into view. He's got a gray goatee and looks like he's about fifty years-old.

"All right," Tucker says as he pushes against the wall. "Keep your eyes off the lady until she gets her clothes," Tucker warns.

The security guard keeps the flashlight trained on us as we hurry back to where we jumped in.

"I'm warning you," Tucker says, staring at the older man with heated eyes. "One look at her and you'll lose your eyes."

But the man doesn't seem interested in me at all. His flashlight is locked on Tucker's cock as he gets out of the pool.

"Great white shark," he says, rubbing his goatee as he stares at Tucker's dick with wide eyes.

"I don't think you have to worry about me," I say with a giggle as I hurry behind the palm trees and quickly put on my dress.

Tucker's cheeks turn red as he quickly yanks up his pants. The flashlight turns off and the security guard sighs in disappointment.

He turns to me and frowns. "Stay out of the pool. But you, Great White Shark," he says to Tucker, "you can swim naked on my shift anytime."

Tucker hurries over, grabs my hand, and nearly yanks my arm out of its socket as he pulls me away. "Let's get the hell out of here before *he* pulls out *his* handcuffs."

CHAPTER FIFTEEN

DAY FIVE

Tucker

I thread my fingers through Julia's silky dark hair and make a fist as her lips squeeze my shaft tight. Her lips feel like heaven. Her tongue feels paradise.

This is my favorite way to wake up in the morning.

I woke up to a soft wet tongue sliding up and down my shaft. I thought it was a dream, but when I opened my eyes it was even better than a dream. It was a reality.

She looks up at me with her sexy green eyes that are watering from my thick cock. She moans as she sinks her head down deep, taking in so much of me that I roll my head back and groan. *Fuuuuucccckk. She is amazing.*

"You like sucking my big dick?" I ask as she slowly pulls up. My cock slides out of her wet lips into her hand.

"I fucking love it," she says, taking a deep breath before taking me into her mouth once again.

I'm breathing heavily as I watch her. My heart is

hammering in my chest as she works me with her delicate little hands and lush lips.

I still can't believe that she's here with me. I always wanted Julia like this, but I never thought I'd get it. I've always wanted her. Since I was six years old and my little sister brought her home to play with Barbies. I've been hooked.

She picks up the pace, hammering my shaft with her tight grip as she traces the tip of my thick head with her tongue.

Seeing her like this, with my cock against her sweet lips, is too much to take and I start feeling the short spasms that always come before I release.

"Just like that," I groan, gritting my teeth as she strokes me even harder. I'm grunting like a caveman as she takes me into her mouth and sucks me so hard that her cheeks hollow.

A savage grunt rips from my throat as I coat her mouth with my hot come. She moans contently as she drinks it down, savoring every last drop.

My head feels like it's filled with lead, and it drops down on the pillow as I try to catch my breath.

She disappears for a few seconds as I stare up at the ceiling, feeling like I just got hit with a tranquilizer dart.

"Here you go, sexy," she says, handing me a steaming cup of coffee. "I'm going to jump in the shower."

I think I'm in love.

But, I already knew that.

I take the cup from her and manage to climb up onto my elbows as I watch her strut into the bathroom. She's wearing only her panties with her long black hair tumbling down her bare back.

"Can I come with you?" I ask, dreading the moment

when she's going to close the door and take away that beautiful ass.

"My pussy needs a break," she says, looking over her shoulder with a grin. "Just a short one."

I take a sip of the coffee as she closes the door, hoping she's not going to take too long. Those scrumptious ass cheeks are painted on the backs of my eyelids, but the real thing is infinitely better.

My head is still spinning, so I place the coffee on the nightstand and drop my head back down on the pillow to recover.

A few minutes later, when the shower water is running, my iPhone starts ringing beside me. I reach over and grab it, answering without looking who's calling.

"Tucker."

"*Can I speak to Miss Julia Tanner?*" the voice asks.

Julia? Huh?

I pull the phone away from my head and realize that I picked up hers by mistake.

"She's not available right now," I say, my voice still groggy. "You want to leave a message?"

"*This is the Marion Debt Payment Group,*" he says. "*She hasn't returned any of our calls. Do you know when she'll be available?*"

"Debt Payment Group?" I mutter. "What is this concerning?"

"*The twenty-nine thousand dollars that she owes us,*" he says, sounding frustrated.

Twenty-nine grand?!? My little sexpot likes to spend money. I wonder how she's going to pay that off with a kindergarten teacher's salary.

"Email me all of the information," I say, giving him my email address. "I'll see what I can do."

"Tell her to call me immediately," he says, sounding bitter. *"Our company will take her to court if she defaults again."*

"Just send me the information," I snap back. "You deal with me now."

I hang up on the little prick and place her phone back on the nightstand. I grab my coffee and walk over to the closet where all of her clothes are hanging up.

A quick rifle through her dresses and it tells me everything I need to know. Prada. Givenchy. Oscar De La Renta.

She has a dozen sunglasses from Derek Lam to Linda Farrow. Same with her shoes: Christian Louboutin. Manolo Blahnik. Valentino.

"Who were you talking to?" she asks when the water shuts off a few minutes later.

"I was just looking in the mirror and telling myself how good I look."

She laughs as she rolls her eyes. "I shouldn't have asked. Want to hit the gym before breakfast?" she asks as she dries off her perfect body.

"Sure," I say as I get dressed. "You go and I'll catch up. I have something to take care of first."

"Everything okay?" she asks me, looking concerned.

"It will be now." I kiss her warm lips, smack her ass, and head for the door.

Mr. Mastercard and Mr. Visa have been her Sugar Daddies for too long. Now it's my turn.

Forty-two minutes and almost a hundred grand later, Julia is out of debt. She doesn't know it yet, but she is.

I had my accountant hunt down every last penny that she owes, and I paid it all off. Every. Single. One.

It took a bit longer than I had thought, so I'm a little late for our gym date. I run through the resort, putting my shoes on as I pass the pool where we got caught last night, and burst through the doors.

Oh, hell no!

Julia is wearing the tightest little shorts and a sports bra (that I now just paid for), doing squats. But that's not what has me puffing my chest out as I hurry over. There are Navy SEALs everywhere, all surrounding her as she squats. Touching her back to spot her, watching her form, admiring her ass. I storm over like an over-possessive gorilla.

"Sorry, I'm late, Julia," I say, elbowing my way in. I lock eyes on each one of the males as I pass them, warning them alpha to alpha that she is mine.

"I'll take it from here," I say, flexing my chest as I step in close to her. One by one, they leave.

"Thanks, guys," she says, smiling knowingly at me. She can sense my jealousy, but I don't care. I just want them to go away. This girl is mine.

"I guess I have to keep a closer eye on you," I say when we're alone by the squatting rack. "I leave you alone for five minutes and you're surrounded by G.I. Joes."

"Jealous?" she asks with a satisfied grin. "Keep that in mind the next time you keep me waiting for *twenty* minutes, not *five*."

"I'll keep that in mind," I say, grinning at her as I pick up some weights. I start warming up my arms as she takes the weights off her bar. "Do you attract one guy for every minute I'm late? Is that how it works?"

"When I'm all sweaty at the gym," she says with a chuckle. "When I'm all dressed up, it's usually two guys a minute."

"You won't be mad at me when you find out what I was doing," I say, excited to tell her the good news.

"Oooh," she says, smiling as she takes off the last weight. "I'm listening..."

"I answered your phone by mistake when you were in the shower," I say.

Her body tightens. "Okay," she says nervously. "Who was it?"

"I think you know who it was."

Her eyes drop to the floor and her ears turn red with embarrassment. "I'm going to pay them all back."

"You don't have to," I tell her. "You don't owe them anything. Not anymore."

Her eyes dart up to mine. "What?"

"I took care of it."

She thrusts her hands onto her hips. "What do you mean you took care of it?"

"I paid all your bills. What? I thought you'd be happy."

She looks anything but happy. Her green eyes look like they're on fire. "I don't need you to pay my *anything*," she shouts. The other people in the gym start looking over at us.

"Julia," I whisper. "This is a good thing."

"I didn't want you to do that," she says with her nostrils flaring. "I can take care of myself!"

"How were you going to do that?" I ask, getting frustrated. "Six figures of high interest debt? How were you going to pay that?"

"That was for me to figure out," she shouts. She grabs her towel and yanks her water bottle off the bench. "So what, now I owe you something? You can hold this over my head?"

I put my hands out in a gesture of surrender. "It wasn't like that. I swear."

"Next time mind your own business," she says before spinning on her heels and storming out of the gym.

The Navy SEALs are watching me with satisfied looks on their faces.

I turn away from them and look at myself in the mirror. *I was doing better when I was being an asshole.*

I can't win with this girl.

CHAPTER SIXTEEN

DAY FIVE

Julia

"It's beautiful," I say, smiling at Cynthia as she looks over the area on the beach where she's going to be married tomorrow. The chairs and tables are set up without all of the fancy table cloths, flowers, and other over-priced wedding crap that will be there to make it look even more stunning tomorrow. They'll be married under palm trees, and then we'll be dining with our toes in the sand as we watch the sun set over the ocean.

"You think?" Cynthia asks.

I turn to her with a furrowed brow. "Don't you?"

"Yeah," she says, smiling wide. "It's going to be perfect."

"I can't wait to see you in your dress, all done up," I say, sliding a curly strand of her brown hair through my fingers. "I'm going to want to marry you."

"You'll have to settle for being the maid of honor," she says. "I only want to marry one person."

"You're lucky," I say, hooking my arm around hers. "It's nice to find your soulmate."

Cynthia turns to me with a raised eyebrow. "Maybe you've already found yours. Maybe he's been in front of your face the entire time."

I exhale long and hard. "God help me if it's your brother."

She laughs. "How's it been going between you two? Without any details, please. You seem to be having a good time. It's about time you two realized that you're perfect for each other."

"I don't know if we've realized that yet," I say, feeling my chest tighten when I think back at the gym this morning. I was mad then, but I'm just embarrassed now. It was my darkest secret, and I was completely humiliated when I found out that he knew.

Tucker is at the bar talking with Lucas. I've been avoiding him all day. It's getting harder to stay away from him now that the rehearsal dinner has started and we're only a dozen people, but I'm up for the challenge. I still can't face him yet. He probably wants to dump me, thinking I'm going to spend all his money.

"Are you nervous for tomorrow?" I ask, trying to change the subject.

"I wouldn't be nervous if Stephanie wasn't here," she says, looking around for the super cunt. "I just wish that she would do whatever she's planning already and get it over with. This waiting and not knowing is killing me."

"What can she possibly do?" I ask with a shrug of my shoulders. "We've foiled any attempt that she's tried to sabotage us in the past."

"She wasn't engaged to the owner of the resort for Megan's wedding," she says with a shiver. "She didn't have the staff listening to her every command for Tanya's wedding. I bet she learned a bunch of tricks while she was in prison. Tricks she's going to use on me."

"I think you're being paranoid."

"Am I?" she says with a huff. "She's already upped her psychological warfare game. This laying low is worse than anything. She's making me lose my mind."

"Maybe she's grown as a person," I say, trying to make her feel better. "Maybe she really is in love with Lars and has changed her ways."

Cynthia gives me a look. She's not buying it.

"Yeah, she's planning something," I say with a nod. "But don't worry. We'll all be on our toes for it."

"Thank you," she says as she leans her head on my shoulder. "I can always count on you bitches."

The wedding coordinator calls us all over and begins to explain what we have to do tomorrow and where we'll have to go. Unfortunately, Tucker is in the wedding party on the groom's side. I'm sure that Chase wants him here even less than I do.

The guys and girls pair up as we practice walking down the aisle. Chase and his best man Ethan are standing at the altar.

Megan jumps on Tucker's arm. "Shotgun, Tucker," she says with a grin.

Lucas looks upset until Tanya grabs his skinny arm. "Don't worry, Lucas. I'll be your girl," she says.

Megan turns around and playfully elbows her husband. "Good for you, honey. Look at the size of her tits."

He starts turning red as Tanya rolls her eyes.

I stand behind the two couples by myself. I'll walk alone as the maid of honor, followed by the bride and her mother. Cynthia made her promise to leave her iPad behind.

"The music will start," the wedding coordinator says, waving her hands, "and then you'll start walking."

She guides each couple along the sandy aisle until it's my turn. Tucker's eyes are locked on me, but I keep mine straight ahead. I'm still too embarrassed to look him in his gorgeous eyes.

"And now the bride," the wedding coordinator says, waving Cynthia and her mom forward when I step onto the low stage.

Of course, Megan and Tanya both start singing, alternating lines as the bride walks down:

Here comes the bride
 Chase, you better run and hide
 Why is she wearing white?
 Do they expect us to believe that shite?
 I'm sorry Chase she lied
 You're not getting a virgin bride.

Cynthia is laughing all the way up. "I hope you got that out of your system, because there will be no singing at the ceremony tomorrow," she warns.

"Awww," Megan says, slumping her shoulders. "No fair."

"Not even during the signing?" Tanya asks, looking frazzled. "We've been practicing all week."

"You can sing it to me after the ceremony," Cynthia says. "How about that?"

"Excellent," Megan says, pumping her fist in excitement.

The wedding coordinator walks us through the rest of the ceremony and then takes the bride and groom away to show them where the pictures will be taken.

"I'm getting a drink," Megan says, running away.

"I'm getting some shade," Tanya says, hurrying under some palm trees.

My chest tightens when I see Tucker making his way over to me. I can't avoid him any longer.

"You can pay me back if you want," he says, looking upset. He stops in front of me and lowers his head. "What did I do wrong?"

My ears start to heat up again. "I don't need your charity."

"It's not charity," he says, looking like he's sick to his stomach.

"Then what is it?"

"It's me helping a person that I care about deeply," he says with a sigh. "You're stressed about it."

"I'm not stressed about it," I lie. "I have everything completely under control."

He tilts his head and looks at me with a look of disbelief.

"Okay, maybe I'm a little stressed, but I was going to pay it all back."

"I'm sure you were," he says. "But I don't like to see you stressed, or sad, or upset, or anything but happy. And I have the resources to take that stress away, so I did. I would do it again and again in an instant."

"You might have to if I get my credit cards back. I'm kidding," I say after he laughs.

"Look," he says with his hands out. "I'm sorry that I didn't tell you, but I thought you would say no. I'm happy to do it. I just want you to be happy. Are you happy?"

I nod. "I'm happy."

"Me too," he says, reaching for me.

I lean in and let him swallow me in his big muscular

arms. He smells so good. Like sex and money. My two favorite things.

"But it's a lot of money," I say, resting my cheek on his chest. "I feel bad."

He gently grabs my arms and holds me out so he can look into my eyes. "I'll tell you what," he says with a grin. "When I visit you in Buffalo, you try on all of those sexy outfits for me and we'll call it even. That will be worth every last cent."

I smile shyly. "I can start with the bikini collection when we get back to the room."

He grins as he looks at me with hungry eyes. "Did I buy you any lingerie?"

"Not yet," I answer with a laugh.

He pulls me back into his embrace and smiles. "We'll have to change that. *Really* soon."

The rest of the dinner goes great. We have a delicious dinner on the beach with tons of good food and fine wine. I'm sitting next to Tucker and surrounded by my girls at the large round table. Tucker has us laughing as he tells us stories of his Uncle Jack, the military man who raised him.

On his first night living there, Tucker woke up in the middle of the night to the sound of an electric razor. His crazy Uncle Jack held him down and shaved off his mohawk, giving him a more respectable military style buzz cut. I wish I could have seen it in person.

Chase stands up when the dessert is served, a delicious-looking chocolate cheesecake that my fork easily sinks into.

"You don't know how grateful Cynthia and I are to have you all here with us on this special week," he says with his wine glass in his hand. He looks at each member of the wedding party sitting around the table and smiles. "You are the closest people in our lives, and the week wouldn't be the same without any of you."

Tucker drops his eyes and stares into his lap.

"When I first met Cynthia," Chase continues, "I was a mess. My knee was broken, my heart was shattered, and I had no reason to live. My brother and I were constantly fighting, I had no place to call home, and the only thing that mattered to me, the Navy and all of the people in it, had just given me my walking papers. I was ready to die. I had given up."

He takes a deep breath as he fights back tears. "And then," he says, turning to his bride, "you walked into my life and everything changed. You healed my heart. You gave me a reason to live, to laugh, and a reason to love again. Your unbelievable love helped my brother and my relationship become stronger than ever. You gave me a home, one with more love then I ever thought possible. You helped me get back on my feet, despite my broken knee, and not only made my life worth living again, but made it even better than before."

I can see the intense love radiating out of Cynthia's face as she watches her man with glossy eyes.

"You'll never know how much you mean to me, baby," he says, starting to get choked up. He tries to fight back tears, but a few of them come sliding down his cheeks. "You are everything to me. *Everything*. And I'm so happy that I get to marry you tomorrow, Cynthia." He shakes his head as he stares at her in disbelief. "We'll be married forever, but I still can't wait. Forever is a long time, but with you by my side, it will feel like an instant. I can't wait to share every moment with you. To live every day with you. To watch you grow old and gray, and still see the young girl that I fell in love whenever I look into your eyes. Enjoy your last night as a bachelorette, Cynthia. Because tomorrow you're mine, and I'm never going to let you go."

Cynthia jumps up and leaps into his arms as the table cheers and wipes away the tears from their eyes. They're holding each other so tight as Chase whispers something in her ear just for her.

I look up at Tucker and jerk my head back in surprise when I see his eyes wet.

"Are you okay?" I whisper when he looks at me.

He gives me a quick nod and turns away as the bride and groom sit back down.

"I second everything that Chase just said, but for this chocolate cheesecake," Megan says, licking her fork. "I'm in love."

Everyone laughs and then starts digging into the dessert. The conversations start going again, and I'm about to ask Tucker what he's thinking when Tanya leans in from my other side.

"First fight as a couple?" she whispers.

"One of many, I'm sure," I answer with a laugh. "We're both stubborn and are bound to butt heads again, but as long as we're quick to make up, it will be fine."

She smiles as she takes a bite of her cake. "So, everything is okay now?"

"Yeah," I say, smiling nice and wide. "Everything is great." I look around to make sure that no one is listening and then lean in close to her. "He paid all of my debt," I whisper.

"Shut up," she says, a little too loud. We wait until everyone stops looking at us. "All of it?"

"All $98,456.19 of it," I whisper. I still can't believe it. It would have taken me half a decade, working four jobs to pay that off.

"Wow," she says, nodding at me like she's impressed. "He must be really in love."

A smile breaks out across my lips. "I think he always was."

"Have you talked about what's going to happen?"

"With what?"

"He lives in Minneapolis," she says. "Last time I checked you lived in your parent's basement in Buffalo."

I gulp. "I didn't want to think about that. I've just been enjoying the moment."

"Well you should," she says, taking a bite of her cake. "God, this is so good. You have tomorrow left together, and then we're leaving."

I take a long gulp of my wine, trying to push the horrible thought out of my head. *We have tonight too.* I'm trying to stay positive.

I reach over to put my hand on his leg, but I touch nothing but air. His chair is empty. After a quick scan of the beach, I see him talking to Chase by the bar.

"I'm going to grab a drink at the bar," I say to Tanya. "Want something?"

"Yeah, I'll take a lemonade with a side of eavesdropping," she says with a grin.

"Shut up," I say to her with a laugh as I get up. I hurry over, keeping far enough away to look inconspicuous but close enough that I can hear.

"I'll take a mojito please," I tell the bartender. I hate them, but they take forever to make. It will allow me to listen for a little longer.

"You're right," I hear Tucker say, "and I'm sorry. I really was acting like a dick."

"Don't sweat it," Chase says. "It's okay."

"It's not," Tucker answers. "I should have given you the benefit of the doubt, but I didn't. I see now that you love her. I can see now that you're a good guy. I just wouldn't let myself see it before."

"Here you go," the bartender says, handing me the mojito.

Shit. I have to get the fastest bartender in all of Aruba.

"I'm allergic to mint leaves," I say as I scrunch up my nose. "Can you make another one please?"

The bartender gives me a weird look and then takes the drink away, shaking his head as he grabs another glass.

"My dad ran out on us before Cynthia was walking," Tucker explains. "I've always been protective of my little sister. She didn't have a dad to look out for her, so I had to be it for her. I tried but I was young, and I didn't always do it the right way."

"Here you go," the bartender says, rolling his eyes as he hands me the drink. "A mojito without the most important ingredient."

Crap. Is this guy the frigging Flash?

I still want to listen so I slide the glass back. "Oops. I forgot to say no ice. I'm allergic."

He takes a deep breath and then takes the drink back, muttering something under his breath as he grabs a spoon to take out the deadly ice.

"We're on the same side, Tucker," Chase says, placing a hand on Tucker's shoulder. "Cynthia has both of us looking out for her now."

"Us two and a group of Navy SEALs?"

"A whole *army* of Navy SEALs," Chase says with a laugh.

"One mojito, no mint leaves, no ice," the bartender says, slapping it down in front of me.

"And no sugar, right?" I ask with an ear still on the boys.

"No sugar?" the bartender says, staring at me in disbelief.

"That's what I ordered."

"That is definitely one hundred percent *not* what you ordered," he says, glaring at me.

"I'm on a sugar-free diet," I say with a shrug.

"Of course you are," he says, taking the glass and turning around to make another one.

I turn back just in time to see Chase and Tucker hugging it out. I'm so relieved to finally see them getting along. I know how much they both mean to Cynthia, and I want tomorrow to go perfectly, not just for her, but for everyone.

"What did you really have in the poker game?" Chase asks with a raised eyebrow.

"A pair of twos," Tucker lies.

Chase laughs and smacks his back. "You're not as good a liar as you think you are. I saw Julia's face when you folded."

Tucker whips his head around to me, and I drop my eyes to the sand with a gulp.

"One mojito," the bartender says, taking a deep breath as he places the drink down in front of me. "No mint leaves, no ice, and no sugar. Is this okay or would you like me to make it without a glass?"

"This is fine," I say, feeling my cheeks redden as Tucker walks over.

"What are you drinking?" Tucker asks, taking the drink from my hand. "Ugh!" he says, looking disgusted after taking a sip. "What is that?"

"A mojito," I say, trying to keep my eyes off the bartender who's still standing there.

Tucker shoots him a look. "That's the worst mojito I've

ever had," he says, handing the glass back to him. "Let's go finish our wine."

I cringe as I glance back and see him shooting daggers at me as Tucker pulls me away.

We sit down at the table and eat our cake as the DJ starts playing some fun dance music. "So," I say, trying to stop my cheeks from turning red. "You said you were maybe potentially going to come and visit? Is that still on the table?"

"That is *definitely* on the table," he says, locking his sexy eyes on me.

"When would that be?"

"We get back on Saturday," he says, looking out at the ocean. "How about Sunday?"

I laugh so suddenly that I almost spit wine out of my nose. I'm really happy that I don't.

"That sounds good," I say as I dig my fork into my cake. "But I'll probably still be on my layover in Colombia."

"No, you won't," he says with a shake of his head. "I'll upgrade you to a direct ticket."

I exhale as I shake my head. "I think you've done enough."

"I can never do enough for you," he says.

I smile shyly, watching as my friends start dancing on the beach. "Come," I say, taking his hand. "Dance with me, Mother Tucker."

He tosses his napkin on the table and stands up with a smile on his face. "Whatever you say, Mosquito Bites."

"Yes!" Megan shouts as we dance over to join the group. The DJ is playing all 90s Hip Hop, arguably the best music ever made.

2Pac and Dr. Dre come through the speakers rapping their classic track, *California Love*, and we all go nuts. Ethan is rapping into Tanya's pregnant belly while she throws her hands in the air.

Megan is grinding on Lucas, using his skinny body like a stripper pole while Cynthia does the running man next to Chase, who is doing the worm in the sand. Tucker's mom is dancing too, holding her iPad up as she films it all.

Tucker is a surprisingly good dancer, and we get in nice and close while moving to the beat.

"I'm getting married tomorrow!" Chase shouts, and we all cheer as the music and drinks flow.

The wedding tomorrow is going to be a blast.

As long as we can keep the new owner of the resort at bay...

CHAPTER SEVENTEEN

DAY SIX

Julia

"What the hell?" I shout in a panic. I spring up in bed, looking around in confusion as someone runs across the room.

The curtains are ripped apart, and the bright Caribbean sun shines into the room as Cynthia throws her head back. "Thank God!" she shouts, taking a breath of relief. "Not a cloud in the sky."

"Great," I say, dropping my head back onto the pillow. "Can you close the curtains now before I go blind?"

She just ignores me and runs over, squealing as she jumps onto my bed. "I'm getting married today!" she says, bouncing up and down.

"You can't get married if you're dead," I warn her.

"Looks like my maid of honor needs some coffee in her system," she says as she climbs off the bed and heads for the tiny coffee machine on the dresser.

"You just saved your own life," I mutter, rubbing my eyes.

"I was so worried it would be raining," Cynthia says as she pours a bottle of water into the machine.

"It still would have been perfect if it was raining," I say, running my hand through my hair as I sit up.

"Sure, sure, but the sun is much better," she says, smiling as she looks out the patio doors.

I glance behind me at the wall that separates my room from Tucker's. I'd much rather wake up with his naked muscular body beside me, but keeping the bride away from the groom on her wedding day is one of the maid of honor's duties, and I wasn't about to let my girl down.

Besides, the way things are going, I'll have the next few weeks, months, or maybe even years to wake up beside him.

Cynthia starts the coffee and then checks on her dress that's hanging in the closet.

"I can't wait to see you in that," I say, smiling as I watch her. She's got an excited nervousness radiating off her. She's so cute.

"I can't wait to see Chase's face when he sees it," she says, taking a deep breath. "I hope he likes it."

"He'll like it."

"All right," she says, checking herself in the mirror. "No zits, check. No rain, check. No stolen dress, check."

"Coffee, check," I say, getting out of bed when the coffee is finished.

"Everything is going to go smoothly," she says, telling me or the reflection in the mirror, I'm not sure. "I guess Stephanie won't try anything. She's been strangely quiet all week, so maybe that means she's changed her mind."

"For sure," I say, not believing that for a second. That bitch is definitely going to try something.

"Everything is going to go off without a hitch," she says, smiling nervously.

I glance back at the wall, wondering what Tucker is doing behind there as Cynthia shows me how she's going to wear her hair. She tries to hold all of the wild curls over her head, but they keep falling. Nothing a few bottles of hair spray and an army of clips can't handle.

My mind is on Tucker as she rambles on about all of the decorations and flower arrangements. I can't help wondering if he meant what he said last night. Is he really going to come and visit me in Buffalo, or will I be long forgotten once we get home and fall back into our usual routines?

I can go and visit him now that my debt is repaid. I can save up for a plane or bus ticket and go see him if he wants me to. I definitely won't be shopping like I used to anymore. I finally realized that all the shopping was just me trying to fill a hole in my heart—a hole that Tucker fills perfectly. I was always in love with him, but I just didn't want to admit it.

"Want a coffee?" I ask the bride while she poses to the reflection in the mirror while holding her hair up.

"Nah," she says before puckering her lips. "I don't want my teeth to be yellow for the pictures."

I sigh and then head into the bathroom.

"Where are you going?" she asks.

"To dump my coffee," I say with a sigh. "And to brush my teeth."

There's a knock on the door just as I'm about to pour my coffee into the sink and watch the delicious black liquid swirl down the drain.

"Is that going to be my brother?" Cynthia asks.

"I hope so," I say, skipping as I hurry to the door.

"Make sure he's dressed if you let him in here."

I grin at her over my shoulder as I grab the door handle. "I'm not making any promises."

I make a sexy pose as I open the door and then quickly straighten up when I see two security guards standing in the hall. I recognize one of them. He was the one watching Home Improvement when I arrived. I narrow my eyes on him. "Yes?"

"Good morning," the other one says. He's rubbing his palms nervously. "There have been some complaints directed toward your group."

My heart starts hammering in my chest. *Is this about the late-night skinny dipping?*

"Unfortunately, you and your group will no longer be staying at the Alanda resort," he says.

My jaw drops.

Cynthia jumps up and rushes over, looking as white as her wedding dress. "Is this some kind of cruel joke? I'm getting married today."

He frowns. "Not on the Alanda resort, you're not. You and your entire wedding party have been banned from the premises. You have thirty minutes to collect your things and bring them to the lobby or the police will be called to escort you out."

I open my mouth to retort, but only a defeated breath comes out. It feels like I got punched in the stomach.

"I don't understand," Cynthia says, holding her temples like this is a bad dream. This is worse than a bad dream. It's a real-life nightmare. "Why are you doing this to us?"

We know why.

"We've been great guests," she says. Her voice is racing. Her hands are shaking. "Who the hell complained?"

Stephanie walks into view with a huge grin on her face.

I lunge at her, trying to rip her face off, but the two security guards catch me and throw me back.

"I told you dirty cunts that I would win," she says, staring at us with her chin thrust in the air. She has a big triumphant smirk on her face. "No wedding beach for you, *Sin*thia. You can get married in the parking lot of the airport where you belong."

"You can't do this," Cynthia says, fighting back tears. She's shaking her head, probably trying to wake up from this nightmare.

Stephanie's grin turns into a wide smile. Her evil eyes are sparkling. "Oh, yes, I can do this. I *am* doing this. You ruined my wedding, and now I'm going to ruin yours."

"I wasn't even at your wedding, you psychotic bitch!" Cynthia screams. Her hands are squeezed so hard into fists that her knuckles are white. So are mine.

Stephanie crosses her arms over her chest and grins. "I saw you and Chase standing on your balcony, laughing at me as I walked out of my wedding."

"*Escorted* out," I correct. "In handcuffs. After your groom ran away."

Her heated eyes dart onto me, and a cold shiver snakes through my body. "I'm going to be Mrs. Lars in a few weeks. This is my resort now."

"Mrs. Lars?" I ask. "Do you even know his last name?"

"It's Dutch or something," she says with a shrug. "Nobody can remember those stupid last names. They're just a string of vowels with a bunch of K's and J's thrown in."

"Wow," I say, rolling my eyes at her. "It sounds like you're really in love."

"*He's* really in love," she says, glaring at me. "And that's all that matters."

"Does he know that you're only marrying him so you

can sabotage my wedding?" Cynthia asks, sounding a little panicked.

"He'll find out soon enough," she says with a shrug. "When you are back in Buffalo, New York, placing your wedding photo on your fireplace mantel. The photo where you're standing beside a dumpster in the Aruba airport, crying over your destroyed wedding."

I lunge at her again, but strong hands catch me and push me back.

She just laughs as I nearly fall to the floor.

"You have thirty minutes to vacate," the security guard says.

Stephanie's lips curl up into an evil smile. "Give them fifteen minutes. Their smelly cunts are stinking up the room."

She's about to walk away when she turns and sees the wedding dress hanging on the wall. "A hideous dress for a hideous bride."

This time the guards are too slow, and I manage to punch her in the tit before they grab me and throw me back into the room.

"Fifteen minutes," the security guard says before slamming the door in my face. "Or we're calling the police."

CHAPTER EIGHTEEN

DAY SIX

Tucker

My pulse is racing as I pace around the lobby with gritted teeth. All of the wedding party is sitting in the lobby with their hastily packed suitcases. Some people look like they just got up. Lucas is still in his pajamas.

"Let me go!" Megan screams as Ethan, Julia, and Lucas struggle to hold her back. Her skin is a fiery red, and she's got murder in her eyes. "I'll rip every strand of her hair out, one by one!"

Cynthia and Chase look miserable as they knock on the owner's door. I hurry over to join them. If the owner wants more money, then I'll happily pay to stop him from ruining my sister's important day. I can't help but feel partly responsible since I was the one who invited Stephanie here in the first place.

Although, I did uninvite her, and something tells me that she would have showed up no matter what. Even if I'd never met her.

Chase opens the door and barges in when he doesn't answer. "I'm busy," Lars says, jumping out of his seat. "Please leave my office at once."

"You're not hiding in here," Chase says, storming up to him with fire in his eyes. "You owe us an explanation. We're paying customers!"

Lars gulps as he backs away from the muscular man in front of him. "You'll get a full refund for the wedding and half of your money back for the week."

"That's not good enough!" Cynthia shouts. "I'm supposed to be getting married. Today! Why are you people doing this to us?"

Chase pinches the bridge of his nose, trying to control his temper. "Look. Stephanie is my cousin. I've known her since she lit her parent's garage on fire. You don't know what you're getting yourself into, man. She's nuttier than squirrel shit. She's certifiably insane!"

"That's my fiancée you're talking about," Lars says, trying to play the tough guy, but one look at Chase's furious face has him cowering backward.

I step forward, trying to calmly explain. "She dated me under a fake name just so she could get invited here to ruin the wedding. I'm sorry, Lars, but she doesn't care about you."

He's not buying it. "We're in love," he says, staring at me with hearts in his eyes.

These two deserve each other.

Cynthia slams her fist onto the desk, glaring at him like a crazed gorilla. "Stephanie is incapable of love," she screams. "She's pure evil in human form. She will eat you alive. Why can't you see that?!?"

Lars straightens his back and lifts his chin in the air. "Our decision is final," he says in a firm voice. "My fiancée wants you out, you're all out."

Cynthia is turning green as she stares at him. Either she's going to turn into the She-Hulk, or she's going to puke all over the desk.

It's the latter. She vomits all over his laptop and the papers on his desk.

"Your bus is here," Lars says, cringing as he steps away from the puke. "It will take you anywhere you want to go on the island."

"Oh, thanks," Chase says as he holds Cynthia's shoulders. He starts guiding her to the door. "Where the hell are we supposed to go?"

"I suggest the airport," Lars says. "Most resorts are fully booked this time of year."

Chase just shakes his head as he opens the door. Julia comes running to get the sick bride. She gives me a concerned look before helping her walk away.

"Shit," Chase mutters when we're outside of the office. He looks at me with blank eyes. "What the hell am I supposed to do?"

I pull out my phone and point to the bus. "Just grab a seat and take care of your girl. *I'll* take care of this."

"You want me to get married at a nudist resort?" Cynthia asks, staring at me in disbelief.

"No one will be naked," I say, swallowing hard. *I hope.*

"Except maybe Irving and Yanina," Julia adds.

"Who?"

Uh-oh. She looks like she's going to puke again.

I glance out the window of the bus at the thick vegetation. We pass the spot where my rental car broke down and it's gone. Either the rental car company got it going again, or the huge insects living in the rainforest devoured it.

"I'm getting married in a nudist resort," Cynthia says, staring at the roof of the bus. "This can't be happening."

"Trust me, Cynthia," I say, putting a hand on hers. "Do you trust me?"

"I trust you," Chase says, locking eyes on me.

"Thank you. I won't let you two down."

I hope.

"This is it?" Cynthia asks when we finally arrive at the Sunnyside Resort. "But there are no naked people."

"I told you," I say with a hard swallow. Hopefully Yanina and Irving haven't booked any guests in the past few days who will ruin the wedding photos.

"It's a beautiful spot," she says, looking around at the sun sparkling over the turquoise water. "But there are no tables or chairs or food or anything."

"Not yet," I say, grabbing her arms. "But I have a few hours and a team of Navy SEALs at my disposal. It's going to look great."

She's biting her bottom lip as she looks around, but she's nodding and looking less stressed than I've seen her all day.

"Come," Julia says, hooking her arm around my sister's. "Tucker called and reserved the entire inn. We'll all have to share rooms, but it will be fun. Like we're back at summer camp."

"Don't worry," I say, smiling at her. "You and Chase will have your own room. The biggest one they have."

"Thanks, Tucker," Cynthia says, finally looking better. "It's going to be great."

"It will," Julia says, winking at me. "Megan! Tanya! Would you guys bring up the dresses and makeup?"

"On it!" Megan shouts before darting to the storage area of the bus.

"Let's go get you ready and have some fun," Julia says, pulling her away. She turns and looks at me over her shoulder. "You sure you have this covered?"

"You won't recognize the place," I say confidently, although my stomach is rolling with nerves. I've never planned a wedding before, let alone one in two hours.

Julia smiles at me one last time before bringing the bride to the inn. Yanina is all smiles as she rushes out to greet the girls and show them up to the honeymoon suite.

I find Irving, and we make a quick plan to set everything up. They have all the tables, chairs, and decorations necessary for a wedding in storage, but we'll still be missing flowers, food, and alcohol. Luckily, I know all of the caterers from planning my date with Julia.

Chase walks over, looking relieved. "Nice place," he says with a nod. "Thanks, Tucker."

"Don't thank me yet," I say, grinning as the guys swarm around me. "We have a lot of work to do."

"What do we do, boss?" Ethan asks with his hands on his hips.

I start barking orders at all of them, telling half of the Navy SEALs to get the stuff out of storage and order the other half to start decorating. Luckily, they're used to following orders and do everything I say without complaining.

I send Lucas and Ethan off into the nearby rainforest to pick flowers, and I grab my phone to start making some calls. "I need a DJ with speakers, food, drinks, and a minister."

"I can marry them," Irving says proudly. "I'm an anointed minister. I took an online course."

"Will you keep your clothes on throughout the ceremony?" I ask, pointing my finger at him.

"Just this one time," he answers.

"Sold!"

"What can I do?" Chase asks, rubbing his palms together.

"Your job is the most important," I say, locking eyes on him. "Change into your bathing suit, go into the kitchen, grab a couple of Coronas, and relax by the water. This is your wedding day. You're not doing anything except saying 'I do' and sliding a ring on my sister's finger."

He laughs as I start dialing the phone. "I was all wrong about you," he says, shaking his head.

"That makes two of us," I say, grinning at him as the phone rings. "Hello? Yes! I need a DJ who knows a shit ton of 90's hip hop."

Three hours later and the place looks spectacular. Well, most of it.

"What the hell is that?" I shout, pointing at the ugliest centerpiece I've ever seen.

Lucas shrugs. "I'm a dentist, not a florist. I'm trying my best here."

"This looks like poison ivy," I say, laughing at it. "I said flowers, not weeds."

"We used all of the flowers for the bridal bouquets," Lucas whines. "I'm not going back in there. I was eaten alive by mosquitoes."

"It looks great," Chase says, nodding in approval.

"See?" Lucas says, looking exhausted. "The groom likes it. They're staying."

Luckily, the Navy SEALs take much more pride in their work. The place really does look spectacular. The head table is set up facing the ocean with smaller round tables for the guests in front of it. The chairs are decorated with white cloth and ribbons, and the tables look gorgeous with white table cloths, fancy dinnerware and the mediocre center-pieces that Lucas put together.

They'll be married under a beautiful arch in front of the water on the flat rocks. Cynthia is going to love it.

I check on the DJ who is setting his speakers up in the corner. "You're sure you know 90s hip hop?" I ask, grilling him for the third time.

He nods. "I've got it all from Coolio to TLC to Salt-N-Pepa."

"What about the Notorious BIG?"

"Who?" he answers. "Kidding, kidding," he says when he sees my panicked face. "I have you covered."

I hurry into the kitchen to check on the caterers. There's about a dozen cooks and waiters in there preparing the appetizers and the desserts. There's five crates of live lobsters on the floor which will be cooked when it's closer to dinner.

"Are we on schedule?" I ask the head boss.

"Ahead of schedule," he replies.

I hope so. I'm paying these guys enough. They could sense my desperation on the phone and charged me a *large* fortune for the last-minute service. Oh well, as long as Cynthia is happy, it's worth it.

I head back outside and make sure the bar is stocked (it is) before going to check on the girls.

"It's Tucker," I say after knocking on the door.

I hear giggles than footsteps before the door creeps open. It's Julia. Her makeup is done and she's dressed up in her baby blue bridesmaid dress. I gasp when I see her, not expecting that.

"Oh, man," I say, swallowing hard as I look her up and down. My heart is pounding like a jackhammer as I try to find the words that will tell her how beautiful she is, but all I can do is stare with my mouth hanging open. There are no words to describe her. She's beyond this world.

"You are magnificent," I say as I drink her up with my eyes. It's not enough, but I still have to say something. "You look stunning."

It seems to be enough for her. She's got a smile from ear to ear.

"How is it looking out there?" Tanya asks.

Julia lets the door swing open, and I get a pain in my chest when I see my beautiful little sister all done up in her wedding dress. My throat burns as my eyes well up.

"Wow," I gasp, staring at her in disbelief. My little sister is all grown up. She's a gorgeous woman now. "It's not looking as good as in here."

The girls laugh as I step in. "Cynthia. You look beautiful. You all do."

"Did you come to hang out with the girls?" Julia asks with a grin.

"We have wine," Megan says, holding up the almost empty bottle. She closes one eye and peers into the bottle with the other. "Well, we did."

"We'll hang out soon enough," I say. "Can you ladies be downstairs in an hour?"

"It's a date," Julia says, smiling up at me.

"Good luck, girls," I say before heading back to the door. "And Cynthia. Absolutely stunning. Chase is a lucky guy."

"Now out!" Julia says, pushing me out the door.

I step into the hallway, grab her arm, and pull her out with me. She grins as I pull her in for a kiss.

"You're amazing," she says when we pull away. "I can't believe you saved this wedding."

"That's what big brothers are for. I even got Yanina and Irving to promise to keep their clothes on."

Julia laughs. "I'll believe it when I see it."

I give her one last smile and then head for the stairs.

"Tucker," she says, following me down the hall. "You said we only have to be downstairs in an hour?"

"Yeah."

She grabs a fistful of my shirt and pulls me into the hall closet. "Good," she says, closing the door behind me and plunging us into darkness. "Then let's get this party started early."

CHAPTER NINETEEN

DAY SIX

Julia

"Good luck," I whisper to the beautiful bride behind me before taking my first step down the aisle. The place really does look gorgeous. Tucker and the boys really did outdo themselves.

I glance at Tanya and Megan who are already under the arch, looking stunning in their bridesmaid dresses. I try to keep my eyes off He-Who-Must-Not-Be-Named because once I look at him, I don't think I'll have the strength to turn away.

A Thousand Years by Christina Perri is playing softly over the speakers as I walk over the flower petals on the aisle past the smiling guests. It doesn't take long for my resolve to crack, and I glance over at Tucker. A flood of warmth flows through me as my breath quickens. He's standing there, back straight, staring right at me with the sexiest honey-colored eyes. He's wearing beige pants with a white button up shirt that hugs his large frame so well that it makes my mouth water. His sleeves are rolled up, showing off his thick inked-up forearms. My mind is two-thirds focused on him, one-third focused on not falling. Cynthia chose thin black ties and thin black suspenders for the guys, and I must say, they look spectacular. On Tucker, anyway. I still haven't managed to pry my eyes off of him to look at the other guys on the platform.

"Wow," Tucker mouths when my eyes finally crawl up to his tanned face. I turn away shyly, smiling at Chase and Ethan, who are looking pretty fine too. Chase is looking delicious in his Navy uniform beside Ethan who is dressed like Lucas and Tucker.

Chase gives me a wink and a smile as I step onto the platform, standing beside Tanya. "Hey, Toots!" I whisper giving her a smirk.

"Looking good, hot stuff," she whispers back.

"This old thing?" I answer, sounding like a good little wife from the 50s.

"Ah," Tanya says, starting to cry already as the music changes to UB40's *(I Can't Help) Falling In Love With You.* "I love this song."

My eyes start burning with happy tears as I watch Cynthia take her first step down the aisle with her mother by her side. She looks perfect with her big curly hair done up over her head, with only a single strand falling down the slender curve of her neck.

I helped pick her dress, a white strapless chiffon wedding dress with a sweetheart neckline. I thought she looked hot in the store, but she's rocking it on another level now with the sun shining down on her shoulders.

The crowd of guests stand up, all smiling and crying as they watch her walk to her soulmate. Chase is holding his breath as he watches her approach, staring at her with hearts in his eyes. His cheeks are glowing and he hasn't blinked once, not wanting to miss one second of this moment.

Her mother looks so proud as she keeps stealing little side glances at her beautiful daughter. She did a great job raising her. I love that girl to death.

I steal a glance at Tucker as his mother gives Cynthia away to Chase. He has a tear in his eye as he watches his little sister move on to the next phase in her life.

"Thank you," Chase says to his new mother-in-law, looking eternally grateful for the precious gift. "I promise to take care of her forever."

"I know you will," Amy says, kissing him on the cheek. "You're a lucky man."

"I was thinking the same thing," Chase whispers to himself as he takes his bride's hand.

Cynthia steps onto the platform and faces her man with a smile on her face. I glance over at Tucker as the music dies down and Irving starts the ceremony.

We hold each other's eyes as Irving rambles on. It's a beautiful ceremony, and for the first time in my life, I want this for myself. I want to get married. I want a wedding. I want a husband. I want Tucker.

I've jumped from boyfriend to boyfriend in the past, never fully committing, because deep down I always knew something was wrong. Something was off. But I never knew what it was until now.

It was that none of the other guys were Tucker.

I can already tell that there will be no more bouncing around from guy to guy. We're going to stay together. We're going to make it work.

He gives me a smile that flows up to his eyes, and I know that he is thinking the same thing.

It's not long before Irving asks the bride and groom for their I Do's. They both eagerly give them, and then he's pronouncing them man and wife.

"You may kiss the bride," he says proudly.

Chase grins as Cynthia jumps into his arms.

"Woooooo!" I cheer, clapping my hands along with the rest of the guests as the two lovers seal their marriage with a kiss.

They finally break apart and hold their hands up for the first time as husband and wife. I couldn't be happier for my best friend. Those two make a great couple, and I know she's going to have an amazing life with her sexy Navy SEAL by her side.

Home by Edward Sharpe & The Magnetic Zeros starts playing through the speakers as Cynthia and Chase dance back down the aisle holding hands. Tucker butts through the rest of the wedding party and joins my side as I follow them down to where the trays of champagne are waiting for us.

"Did I say you look hot as fuck?" he whispers into my ear, making me laugh.

"About a thousand times," I say, smiling shyly.

"Well, here's another one. You look hot as fuck."

I laugh as we arrive at the end where the wedding group is out of their chairs, congratulating the happy bride and groom.

I have to fight back tears when it's my turn. "Congratulations," I say, throwing my hands around Cynthia. Her curly hair tickles my face as she squeezes me tight.

"If I was born a lesbian, I would have married you," she says, kissing my cheek.

"Maybe in the next life," I say with a laugh. "Lucky for Chase, you weren't."

My heart strums happily in my chest when I pull away from my girl and see Tucker hugging Chase. They look like brothers, which is good, because they're brothers now.

Tucker and I sneak away with our champagne as the bride and groom head out with the photographer for some pictures.

I lean my back against a palm tree as he leans over me with his tattooed arm over my head.

"I want to move to Buffalo," he says, taking me by surprise.

"What?" I snort out, nearly spitting champagne all over him.

"I want to move to Buffalo," he repeats. There's no hesitation in his voice.

I look up at him with a raised eyebrow. "You know I'm not going to be dressed like this every day, right?"

"I hope not," he says, looking down at me with a grin. "I'd prefer you naked."

I swallow hard, wondering if he's serious or if he's just caught up in the magical moment of the wedding.

"It's fast," I whisper, staring at the rising bubbles in my glass.

"Does it feel too fast?" he asks in a voice as smooth as leather.

I slowly look up at him and shake my head. "No. It doesn't."

"Then let's do it," he says with a grin. "I think we wasted enough time apart."

I couldn't agree more.

"Okay," I say after taking a deep breath. "This is so crazy."

"Crazy is good," he says with a smile. "We're good. Together we're good."

I look up at him with a mischievous grin. "I'll ask my parents if you can move in."

He laughs. "You let me worry about where we're going to live."

"Deal."

After a record-breaking number of pictures, we finally sit down for dinner. Tucker really pulled through with everything. We're served fresh lobster, rice, and grilled vegetables. And it's freaking delicious.

On my way back from the bathroom, I stop at where he's sitting and lean down close to his ear. "Fresh lobster?" I ask.

He grins. "I always get lucky when I serve you lobster."

"And you always will," I say with a laugh, patting him on his broad shoulder.

I take my seat between the bride and Tanya. The girls are on one side of the head table and the boys on the other. We're overlooking the rest of the guests and facing the spectacular view of the ocean.

"What a spot," Tanya says, smiling as the setting sun shines down on her face.

"This rock is way better than sand," Megan says, tapping the flat rock with her foot. She nods in approval. "Yup. My moves will look way sicker with a firm ground."

"Great," Cynthia says with a laugh. "I wouldn't want any sloppy dance moves to ruin my wedding."

"I completely understand," Megan says with a nod. I can never tell if that girl is joking or not.

Ethan is the MC for the night as well as the best man. He turns on the microphone and weaves his way through the tables. "I'd like to call the bride and groom to the dance floor for the first dance."

We all cheer as Chase helps Cynthia up.

"Have fun," I whisper to her as they walk hand-in-hand to an empty area of the flat rock, which works as a perfect dance floor.

Love Love Love by Of Monsters and Men starts playing softly through the speakers as Chase holds her tight, whispering something in her ear that makes her blush.

"I broke Ethan," Tanya whispers to me. "We're not naming our kid Rocko."

"Thank God," I answer.

"I get to pick the name," she says happily.

"What did you pick?"

"Milhouse," she says proudly. "It was my grandfather's name."

I cringe. It should have died with him.

"I *love* it," Megan chimes in.

I think that poor kid would be better off with Rocko.

The song finishes, and my stomach starts rolling with nerves. It's almost time for my maid of honor speech.

Luckily, Ethan goes first once the bride and groom are seated at the table once again. He stands beside his brother with the mic in his hand.

He thanks everyone for coming and compliments the bride but then starts to get to the good stuff—the stuff that has everyone reaching for their Kleenex.

"Cynthia, I truly believe that you were made for my brother," he says, looking at the bride. "When he came to us in Belize, he was a lost man. *You* grounded him. *You* made him complete. I'm thrilled that my relationship with my brother has never been stronger, and I owe a big part of that to you. Chase was always a man to look up to, a brave hero who fought for his country as a Navy SEAL."

The two tables of Navy SEALs smack the table and cheer. "Hooyah!" they all shout at the same time.

"He was always tough. He was always brave. He always had heart. But you, Cynthia, gave him his true heart. You bring out the softer side to him. The loving side. The side that was always hidden under a rough exterior. I love the both of you so much, and I'm so excited to have a new sister in my life. Congratulations to the both of you."

Chase and Cynthia both stand up and hug Ethan, thanking him for his speech.

"Your turn," Tanya says as my stomach does a cartwheel.

Megan leans over with a grin. "Don't fuck it up," she whispers.

I take a deep breath and stand up. Tucker smiles at me and wishes me good luck with his eyes, and I instantly feel a little better. I always feel better when I know he's here with me.

"Nice speech," I whisper to Ethan as he hands me the mic.

"Good luck," he whispers back before sitting down beside his brother.

Cynthia is watching me with a smile on her face and with excitement in her eyes.

I take a deep breath and get started. "On my first day of kindergarten," I say, biting my lip as I turn to the bride. "I was terrified. I was holding back tears all day wanting to crawl under the table and cry out for my mom."

People let out a small laugh, and I start to loosen up, feeling the nerves drift away with the warm breeze.

"The teacher handed out some little milk cartons, the

ones that are impossible to open, and mine was expired. It was full of chunks and smelled as bad as Megan's dancing."

"Hey!" Megan shouts.

I stick my tongue out at her and turn back to the bride. "That was enough to get the waterworks going, and I started bawling. I cried and cried until the cutest little girl with the wildest hair I'd ever seen walked over and sat down beside me. The tears stopped as I stared in amazement at the untamed brown curls and the adorable little girl who was offering to share her milk carton with me."

Cynthia smiles at the memory. I can still remember it like it was yesterday.

"We took turns taking sips, and eventually I built up the nerve to ask her if I could touch her crazy curls. She said yes, and in that moment my life was changed for the better because those curls were attached to the best person on the planet."

We both start to get choked up as we smile at each other. "We've been through a lot, Cynthia and me. Two and a half decades of being best friends has put us through countless firsts and challenges, but we always come through stronger than ever on the other side. We have millions of memories, inside jokes, embarrassing stories, and secrets, and I cherish every single one of them."

I turn to the handsome groom and smile. "Chase, I hope you know how lucky you are to have this girl." He nods. He knows. "I should be upset at you for taking some of Cynthia's heart from me. But I'm not, because Cynthia has the biggest heart of anyone I know, and she has more than enough love to go around."

I look over the crowd at all of the smiling faces. Cynthia's mother is holding her iPad up, recording every word.

I raise my glass of wine for the final toast:

"So, here's to the lovely pair,
And all of the beautiful love they share,
To the fulfilling of the vows they swear,
To their joint love, affection, and care,
And may their children get Cynthia's crazy hair.
Cheers!"

"Cheers!" the crowd says as everyone raises their glasses and laughs. Cynthia gets up and swallows me in a hug as Chase joins in, hugging me from the side.

"I love you too," she whispers into my ear before kissing my cheek.

I feel great and ready to party now that my speech is done, and I get to let the nerves go.

"Hot *and* articulate," Tucker says over his shoulder as I walk by. "What a catch!"

I roll my eyes and laugh as I walk by him back to my seat.

"Cute speech," Tanya says as I sit down, taking a breath of relief.

"I didn't care for the part about my dancing," Megan says with a frown. "But the rest was pretty damn good."

"Thanks, guys," I say as I take a long gulp of wine and sit back, finally relaxed.

My relaxation doesn't last long when I glance behind us at the road in the distance. Anger and anxiety takes its place when I see an uninvited guest standing next to a white car.

Stephanie is standing there, watching us.

I squeeze my hands into fists as I stand up with my pulse racing.

"Keep Cynthia occupied," I whisper to Tanya through a clenched jaw. The bride doesn't need to know that she's here.

And besides, I want her all to myself.

CHAPTER TWENTY

DAY SIX

Julia

"What in the hell are you doing here?!?" I hiss.

I've never been so mad as I charge up to Stephanie. My knuckles are burning from squeezing my hands into fists so tightly, fists that I want to introduce to her nose.

She doesn't even look at me as I stomp forward ready to kill her. She's staring at the wedding party with a sad face. Her shoulders are drooped and her eyes are blank as she watches Cynthia kiss Chase as everyone clinks on their wine glasses.

"You have some nerve!" I say, stopping an inch from her face.

"They're not upset," she says in a monotone voice. Her eyes look vacant as she stares. She still hasn't even looked at me once. "They're not fighting or sad or yelling at each other. They're smiling. They're actually happy."

"Of course they are," I hiss. I take a step back, watching

her with confusion. "They're in love. You obviously don't know what that is."

"I don't," she says softly. She turns to me, and I'm taken aback by the swell of pain in her eyes. "No one has ever loved me," she says, looking hollow and lifeless. "No guy, not any friend, not my cousins, or my brother. Not even my parents. They always just sent me to my room while they showered Lucas with the love they didn't have for me."

My lips part, but I have nothing to say. I wasn't expecting Stephanie to have feelings, and it throws me off balance.

She turns back to the wedding party and exhales long and slow. "Look at them," she says, looking dumbfounded. "They're so happy. How can I have that?"

I take a deep breath and shake my head. "Basically, you have to act in the exact opposite way of what you've been doing," I tell her bluntly. "Be the exact opposite of the person you are. Whenever you're about to do something, ask yourself, what would my opposite do, and then do that instead. That will be a good start."

What? She wanted to know.

"All I wanted to do was make them miserable," she says. "But it only made me miserable. They're still happy. You guys will always be happy because you have each other. I'm so lonely, Tanya."

"It's Julia."

"I've never had anyone in my corner. I've never had anyone care," she continues. "I realize now that it was all my doing. It's because I'm a shitty person. I don't want to be a shitty person anymore. I want to have fun and laugh and have meaningful relationships like you guys have with each other. I don't want to be me anymore."

She's like the Grinch when he's having his epiphany on Christmas morning. I wonder if her heart is getting bigger like his did, but then I realize that she probably has no heart.

"I'm sorry I did this," she says as her eyes get red. "I'm sorry I tried to ruin the wedding. All three of them. The truth is, I was jealous of your friendship. I've never had a real friend in my life. I seem to repel people."

"You certainly do that," I answer without thinking. "Sorry," I quickly add when I see her face. I don't need to kick the girl when she's down. "But you don't have to be like this any longer. You can learn to be a good person."

She looks at me with hope in her eyes. "How?"

"Well," I say as I take a deep breath. "You can tell Lars how you really feel for starters. You're marrying the poor guy, and you don't even love him."

She shivers as she listens. "He smells like cinnamon all the time," she says, cringing. "And he's always talking about birds. It's creepy."

I open my mouth to encourage her, but I'm interrupted by a car driving up. It's Lars.

"Here's your first test," I say to Stephanie, trying to give her some strength to do what's right. "Break it to him. Gently."

"Stephanie," he says as he steps out of the car. "You shouldn't be here. Come home."

He reaches for her and she jerks her arm out of his reach. "Don't touch me," she snaps.

Lars recoils in confusion.

He does smell like cinnamon.

"You and me," Stephanie says, wrenching off her diamond ring. "Are done."

"What?" he asks, staring at her with devastation in his eyes.

"I never loved you," she says, getting the ring free. "In

fact, I *hate* you." She takes the ring and launches it over the trees, sending it flying into the thick dense rainforest where he'll probably never find it.

"Why are you doing this my morning dove?" he asks as he drops to his knees. He clasps his hands together as tears roll down his cheeks. "Please!"

"You're so pathetic," Stephanie says, shaking her head as she stares down at him in disgust.

He starts crying, painful ugly sobs. "Wait! My beautiful penguin. Wait!"

Stephanie turns and smiles at me. "Thanks, Tanya," she says, looking like a weight has been lifted off her shoulders. "I feel like a better person already."

She's smiling as she walks back to her car. She opens the door and then pauses, turning to me with a happy smile. "I like this new and better Stephanie," she says proudly. "Things are going to change."

She gives me one last smile before getting into the car and peeling away, sending a dirty cloud of dust into Lars' sobbing face.

Well, Rome wasn't built in a day.

I raise my shoulders and smile awkwardly at Lars, whose sobs have now turned into pathetic whimpers.

I'm about to tell him that he's luckier than he'll ever know, but he tried to ruin my best friend's wedding, so fuck him.

I glance back down at the wedding party and gasp when I see that Cynthia is about to toss the bouquet.

"Crap!" I curse as I lift my dress up and sprint down the road.

I'm catching that shit!

I definitely want to be the next one to get married, and I know to who.

CHAPTER TWENTY-ONE

DAY SIX

Julia

After hours and hours of drinking and dancing, Tanya, Ethan, Chase, Cynthia, Lucas, Megan, Tucker, and I are the only troupers left. We're sitting on the rocks by the water, enjoying the beautiful night and the beautiful company.

I have Tucker's arms wrapped around me—exactly where they belong—as he sips champagne straight from the bottle. He hands the bottle to Chase, who is sitting with his new wife looking happier than ever.

"That turned out pretty good," Megan says. She's leaning on Lucas who is lying on the rocks and snoring loudly.

"That turned out amazing!" Cynthia says. She's had a huge smile on her face all night. It's even bigger now that it's loaded with alcohol. "This was truly the best wedding ever."

"After mine," Megan corrects.

"Please," Ethan butts in. "*Ours* was the best." Tanya is in his arms, looking up at him with tired eyes. For a girl who's very preggers, she's hung in there late. She's even outlasted the Navy SEALs who went to bed about an hour ago.

"Wait until mine," I say with a chuckle.

"*Ours*," Tucker corrects from behind me. I squeeze his big bicep and smile.

Cynthia giggles as she looks at us. "I'd never thought I'd see that picture," she says. "It's a nice one."

Tucker kisses the top of my head, sending warm shivers rippling through me.

It's not a picture I ever thought I'd see either, but it's one that I'm going to hold on to for a long time.

The owners of the inn, Yanina and Irving, walk over looking tired but happy.

"Did you all have fun?" Irving asks.

"A blast!" Ethan says, holding up his beer bottle.

"Thank you so much for taking us on last minute," Chase says, looking so thankful that he didn't have to get married in the parking lot of the airport.

"You two really did an amazing job," Cynthia says, clasping her hands together. "We'll name our firstborn after you."

"We're glad it was to your liking," Yanina says, flashing a missing tooth as she smiles at the tipsy bride.

"It was definitely to our liking," Tucker adds.

"Good," Irving says with a nod. We all watch in stunned silence as the older couple starts undressing in front of us.

"Uhhh," I say, staring as Yanina takes off her bra, showing us her saggy coconuts.

"Welcome to the Sunnyside Resort," Tucker says with a laugh.

Cynthia giggles as Irving slides his underwear down, presenting us with the resort's official mascot.

The old naked couple walk hand in hand through our group and into the water for a late-night swim.

Megan is staring at their wrinkled asses. "This is the first wedding I've been too where I've seen a penis."

"Even yours?" I ask her.

Megan laughs as she elbows her snoring husband in the ribs. He doesn't even move. "Especially mine," she says with a roll of her eyes. "He was even drunker at our wedding. I had to use a vibrator to consummate the marriage."

We all start laughing. Tanya slaps Megan's arm as she shakes her head.

"Well," Megan says, standing up. "I'm going in too."

"With a bathing suit, I hope?" Tanya asks.

"Nope," Megan says as she hides behind a tree and gets undressed. "No looking at my jujubes," she says before running into the water with one hand over her chest and one between her legs.

"What is on her ass?" I ask, narrowing my eyes on her white cheeks that are glowing in the moonlight. It looks like a birthmark in the shape of a lightning bolt.

"That would be a Harry Potter lightning tattoo," Tanya says with a laugh.

"I wish I didn't know that," I say with a laugh as she dives into the water.

"Don't be jealous, Julia," Megan says as she turns around. The water is up to her neck, and it's so dark that no one can see anything but the grin on her face.

"That water looks nice," Ethan says, staring at the ocean.

"I'm going in," Tucker says, jumping up.

"Me too!" Cynthia says, jumping up.

"All right," Tanya says, struggling to get to her feet. "Boys get naked on the right. Girls on the left. No peeking."

Tucker laughs as he joins the boys in the trees on the

right. "My sister is over there," he says with a laugh. "I definitely won't be peeking."

We all run into the dark water and join Megan, Irving, and Yanina for a late-night skinny dip.

It's not long before I find Tucker and swim into his arms.

"What a perfect night," I say, looking up at the thousands of stars as his hand slides into mine.

He smiles as he lifts my hand out of the water and kisses the back of it. "The first of many."

He's got that right!

CHAPTER TWENTY-TWO

Julia

I grab a National Geographic from the magazine stand at the airport and flip through it. There's a mummy on the cover with a seventeen-page article on several new Incan mummies just discovered in the mountains of Peru.

"Sounds interesting," I mumble as I flip through it, looking at the disgusting pictures.

Ah, who am I kidding?

I toss it back on the rack and grab the new Vogue, In Style, and Cosmopolitan. The only wrapped up bodies I care about are the ones wrapped up in designer clothes.

I grab the new Vanity Fair as well. It's going to be a long flight all by myself back to Bogota, Colombia, and I'll need something to do while the movie is playing in Spanish. I have a seven-hour layover, and then I'm flying to Dallas, where I'll switch planes, and then finally fly back to Buffalo. I'm kinda regretting not taking Tucker up on his offer to pay for my direct flight. *Oh, well. It's a little late now.*

Maybe one more. I reach for the latest Elle at the same time as someone else and we bump hands.

It's Stephanie.

"Oh," I say, looking up at her in shock.

"Julia," she says, smiling at me.

"You got my name right. Finally."

She wrings her hands together, looking embarrassed. "I just want to apologize to you for yesterday. I really feel horrible for trying to sabotage the wedding. Thank you for helping me see the light. I really am committed to changing now."

"That's good," I say, still keeping my distance from her. This could be a trap. With Stephanie, you never know.

"Let me buy these for you," she says, taking the magazines from my hands. "As a show of goodwill."

"Uh, okay," I say, furrowing my brow as she takes them. She adds the new edition of Elle onto the pile and walks with me to the cash.

I still keep my distance as the cashier rings them up. "$33.42," the young girl says.

Stephanie hands her a credit card and forces out a smile.

"Would you like to donate a dollar to help build an orphanage in Aruba?" the young girl asks with a bubbly voice.

"*Pfff,*" Stephanie scoffs, looking at the girl like she's crazy. "No. Those lazy kids can get jobs like everyone else if they want money." She grabs her credit card back and rolls her eyes at me as she hands me the magazines.

The young girl looks horrified as she stares at Stephanie in disbelief.

I quickly reach into my pocket as Stephanie walks out.

"For the kids," I whisper, tossing a twenty onto the counter.

I follow her out of the store and catch up to her in the hall. "So, does this mean you won't try and ruin my wedding?"

"Of course I won't," she says with a nod of her head. She perks up. "Will I be invited?"

"Uh," I say looking around in panic. "They just called out that they're boarding my plane. Gotta go!"

"I didn't hear anything," she says, looking around in confusion. "Aren't you coming back to Buffalo? We only board in an hour."

"I'm stopping in Colombia first," I say with a tired breath. "Don't ask."

I say a quick goodbye to her and then head over to where my friends are waiting by the terminal. I have to head over to my gate, so it's time for the goodbyes.

I'll see everyone back at home, except for the most important one.

"I have to go," I say, waving to the group who are all lounging on the chairs looking hungover and tired.

"Enjoy Colombia," Megan says with a wave. "Bring me back some of that uncut Colombian yeyo."

"Now it makes sense," Ethan says with a laugh. "She's a drug mule. Julia are you a drug mule?"

"If I was a drug mule, I would be flying first class," I answer, "instead of being next to some stranger who's going to steal my armrest."

Cynthia gets up and gives me a warm hug. "Thanks for everything," she says. "You really made my week. I know you couldn't really afford it, but I appreciate it so much that you came anyway."

"I wouldn't have missed it for anything," I say, squeezing her back. "I would have sold a kidney if I had to. So, I guess I'll see you at home?"

"Not for two weeks," she says with a wide grin.

"What?"

"Tucker gave us a wedding gift," she says barely able to contain her excitement. "Two weeks in Australia. We're leaving in two days!"

"Get out!"

"I'll be surfing with kangaroos!" she says, squealing in excitement.

"Call me when you get there," I say, pointing my finger into her chest. "And go make some Aussie babies."

I say goodbye to Chase and Tanya and the rest of them, but there's one person missing.

"Where's Tucker?" I whisper to Cynthia. I can't leave without saying goodbye, but I really have to get to my gate.

She shrugs. "I'll just tell him you said goodbye. Kidding," she says when she sees my face. "He's waiting for you at your gate."

My horrified face turns into a smile. "Bring me back a boomerang," I say to her before leaving.

I hurry through the airport, excited to see Tucker's face. It's going to be a while before I see it again.

He looks so sexy standing by the gate with his bag slung over his round shoulder. He's wearing a tight black t-shirt that sends dirty thoughts rushing through my head. *I'm going to miss that view.*

"You came to say 'bye."

He smiles at me as he shakes his head. "Not yet."

"What do you mean?" I ask, eying him funny. "My plane is boarding."

He pulls a ticket out of his pocket and shows it to me. *Tucker Connor. Bogota. Colombia.*

I burst out laughing. "You didn't."

"I did," he says with a grin. "You wouldn't let me switch your ticket, but you have no control over mine."

"Lucky me," I say, biting my bottom lip as I admire his tattooed biceps. Those are some arms I definitely wouldn't mind sharing an armrest with.

"Where are you sitting?" I ask, hoping we're beside each other.

"Beside you. In first class."

"What?"

"I figured you wouldn't be too mad if I upgraded us to first class."

I can't help but smile. "I can live with that."

"And the best part is," he continues. "I booked a five-star hotel outside of the airport for our seven hour layover. You'll be wishing it was twelve."

"Perfect." I can't believe my luck with this guy. He's the thing that's perfect. "So, I'll get laid on my layover?"

"That's what they were invented for," he answers with a smirk.

"That's what *you* were invented for," I say, stepping on my toes to give him a kiss.

My heart swells as we kiss in front of the gate. Aruba was fun, but Colombia is going to be even better!

EPILOGUE

Julia

Three months later.

"I can't believe that you bought us a house!" I say, staring at Tucker in disbelief. "I was not expecting this."

My skin is tingling as I look at the beautiful house with the two-car garage and huge windows overlooking the green yard.

"The neighbors may cause some trouble," he says with a laugh. "But we can always ignore them."

"The neighbors are the best part," I say, smiling as I look down the street at Cynthia and Chase's house. Megan and Lucas are on the right of them, and Tanya, Ethan, and their new baby Liam (they decided against Rocko *and* Milhouse —thank God!) live only one street over. We're all within walking distance now.

"I still can't believe you did this," I say, shaking my head as I walk up the green grass (which is now mine!) and look up at the tall tree on the front yard. I touch the trunk and run my fingers over the rough bark. "This tree is ours."

"It sure is," Tucker says with a laugh. "Every single leaf."

I'm in awe as I walk around the property, too nervous to step inside.

The last three months have been pure bliss since Cynthia's wedding. Tucker set up his real estate investments with a property management firm, which freed him up to move anywhere on the planet. Lucky for me he chose my favorite street in Buffalo, New York.

We barely fight anymore, and he's been the perfect boyfriend. Except last Saturday. Last Saturday, he was his old Mother Tucker self, but I don't mind that once in a while. It keeps things interesting.

"Want to see inside?" he asks, holding up a key.

My heart starts racing as I stare at him with wide eyes. "Are you sure it's ours?"

"It has your name on the deed," he says. "Might as well go check it out."

I take a deep breath and walk over, taking the key from his hands. "Are you sure about this?" I ask, giving him one last chance to back out. We've been talking about moving in together for the past few weeks, but I wasn't expecting this. I was dreaming about this, but I wasn't expecting it.

"Will you go open the door already?" he asks with a grin. "I want to show you your closet."

"My closet?" I ask, getting goosebumps. "Is it big?"

"You'll have to open the door to find out."

I rip the keys out of his hands and open the door with shaky fingers. "Wow," I gasp when I swing the door open. The inside is even nicer than the outside.

I have a constant surge of warmth flowing through my veins as I walk through the house admiring the high ceilings, granite countertops, hardwood floors, and huge windows. It's an open layout and perfect for hosting parties with our new neighbors. I can think of a few in particular.

"What do you think?" Tucker asks, leaning against the wall with a grin.

"I think I'm going to rip your clothes off and christen the house right now," I say, looking around the empty house in amazement. "This is incredible. I mean it's not my parent's basement, but it's still nice."

"Wait until you see upstairs," he says with a laugh. "You just might be changing your tune."

"My closet?" I ask with an excited squeal.

He grins as he turns toward the staircase. "Follow me."

Adrenaline rushes through my veins as I follow him up the stairs into the huge master bedroom. There's no furniture in the house, which makes the rooms look even bigger.

I swallow hard when I see two French doors on the far wall. "Is that?"

"Yes," he says with a nod. "It's your new love."

I take a deep breath, shake my hands out, and open the doors.

"Ho. Ly. Shit." It's massive. I mean, *frigging* massive. Even I would have a hard time filling this thing.

I walk into the middle of the room and stretch my arms out. I spin around and don't even come close to touching a wall.

"Do you like it?" he asks with a smile.

"Like is not the word," I say, gulping as I look around at all of the empty racks, shelves, and drawers. "Love is not the word either."

"What is the word?"

I shake my dizzy head. "I don't know."

"You haven't seen it all," he says, pointing to a door on

one of the walls. I was so taken with the monster closet that I didn't even notice the door.

"What's that?" I ask as my hands start shaking again.

Tucker just shrugs. "Open it and find out."

I rush over and open the door with my heart pounding. "No!" I shout, nearly falling to my knees as my legs buckle. I grab onto the door frame for support. There's a second closet, about a third the size of this one but it's floor to ceiling shelves. "Is that for...?" I can't finish the thought.

"Yup," he says, nodding his head up and down. "Even you can't fill that up with shoes."

My eyes start watering as I stick my head in. "You don't know me at all." I've always wanted my own shoe closet. All kinds of dreams are coming true today.

"I'd like to see you try," he says, reaching into his pocket. He pulls out a black American Express card and hands it to me. "The first two walls are on me."

"I can't take this," I say, trying to hand him the card back even though I desperately want to keep it. I won't fill two walls with it, but maybe two shelves.

"Why not?" he asks, sticking his hands into his pockets as I try to hand him the card.

"Because we're not... you know."

"What?" he asks. "Married?"

"Yeah."

He pulls his hands out of his pocket and my heart skips a beat when I see a little blue box in his hand. "Then we'll have to change that," he says. "For the shoes."

I gulp when he drops to a knee and opens the box. The most beautiful diamond ring is staring up at me, begging me to wear it.

"Julia," Tucker says softly. "Will you marry me?"

My thoughts are scattered, and I'm too excited to think

straight, so I just lunge onto him instead, tackling him to the floor.

"Yes," I say, kissing him on the lips. "Yes. Yes. A thousand times yes!"

He slides the ring onto my finger, and I nearly have a heart attack when I see the size of the diamond. It looks even bigger on my hand.

"Where do you want to get married?" he asks, watching me as I stare at my new best friend. *Sorry Cynthia, but diamonds are definitely a girl's best friend.*

"In this closet," I say, smiling as I look around again. "We could definitely fit all of our guests in it."

Tucker laughs. "What about a destination wedding?"

"I think I've had enough destination weddings for one lifetime."

He grins. "I want to get married on the beach."

I smile as I think about it. Seeing Tucker shirtless does always sound mighty tempting.

"All right," I say, sitting in his lap. "We'll talk."

AFTERWORD

BONUS MATERIAL! Join my newsletter and I'll send you a playlist with all of the songs mentioned in each of the three Bad Boys on the Beach books! Rock out with the songs from the wedding ceremonies!

Get the Playlist for the Whole Series!

Sign up at:
www.AuthorKimberlyFox.com/newsletter.html

Check your latest email from Kimberly@authorkimberlyfox.com
for the link if you're already subscribed to my newsletter

***Keep turning the pages to read the first three chapters of The Best Medicine, a hilarious romantic comedy by Kimberly Fox!

CHAPTER ONE

THE BEST MEDICINE

Shane

"You absolutely have to nail this last course," my manager Christopher says as I climb onto my dirt bike.

I take a deep breath to calm my excited nerves as I grip the throttle and squeeze it. Christopher is right. I fucked up the last landing in the semi-finals when my bike slipped in the mud, and if I want to win the Freestyle Motocross gold medal, I have to do something big.

Something only a lunatic would try.

Good thing I'm the right kind of crazy.

We're at the EXXXtreme Motocross Championship, the biggest event in Freestyle Motocross, and this year I'm determined to go home with the medal. I finished second last year, and it's still a sore spot with me. I'm not going to fail again.

Christopher is biting at his lips as he looks up at the

clock. "They're about to announce you," he says, blinking rapidly.

I'm the one about to risk my life doing insane acrobatic stunts on a dirt bike in front of forty thousand people watching in the stadium and another million or so watching at home, and he's the one who's nervous.

"Relax, C," I say as I slip on my helmet. "I got this. I'm going for it."

"For what?" Christopher asks as his face goes pale. "Shane?"

I give him a playful grin as I lean back, completely relaxed. This is my moment. I've got this.

"The Kamikaze Twister. I'm going to do it."

Christopher rubs his sweaty forehead as he closes his eyes, trying to calm his nerves with deep breaths. I'm his only client, so if this goes bad for me, it's going to go bad for him too.

"Shane," he says, sounding breathless. "You've never landed it once in practice."

I grin as I look past him to the huge crowd of people in the motocross stadium. The flashes of cameras, the big screen, the energy of the crowd—it's all making me that much more sure of myself. If I can do it anywhere, it's going to be here in Seattle, the city I live in.

"This is not practice," I say, feeling more confident than ever. "This is where dreams come true."

"Shane," he says as I slap down the visor on my helmet. I rev the throttle, drowning out his negative words with the rumbling sounds of my motor.

I know I can do this. This is the moment I've been waiting for my whole life. The moment where I test myself to see what I'm really capable of. If I pull it off, I'm a hero. If I don't, I might be leaving here in a body bag.

"*Make a big Seattle welcome for Shane Winters,*" the announcer hollers through the stadium speakers. The crowd roars as I ride up to the starting line to complete the last tour of the night.

I'm competing in the Sexy Six. I have to perform six aerial tricks, and the rider with the best scores on style, level of trick difficulty, and crowd reactions wins.

I ride to the top of the ramp and grin as I look at my picture on the huge jumbo screen. I'm soaring through the air at last year's competition in the middle of a Fender Grab, my signature move. Until now.

Next year's competition will have a picture of me completing the Kamikaze Twister—the insane move that's going to win me the gold medal.

The crowd is going nuts as I take one last breath and drop down the dirt ramp with every cell in my body on full red alert.

Adrenaline is pumping through my veins like a broken fire hydrant, but I'm in perfect control as I hit the first jump and complete my signature move, the Fender Grab. The crowd goes nuts as I land it easily and turn toward the second ramp.

I whip around the course, nailing each landing after soaring through the air and twisting my body like a pretzel.

I can hear the crowd over the pounding in my ears as I line up for the last ramp.

"Let's do this," I mutter to myself as I take off at full speed, about to complete my destiny.

I hit the ramp at a breakneck speed, flying up the steep incline as I grit my teeth. It's the last jump. The time to lay it all on the line and win the gold.

My knuckles are burning as I crank the throttle to the max on my way up. The crowd explodes into camera flashes as my tires leave the ramp, and I soar through the air like a motherfucking fighter jet.

Time slows to a crawl.

I don't have to think. My body just reacts.

Turn hips. Release handlebars. Rotate. Faster. Faster. Good. Kick feet up. Dip head. Grab the handleb—

Fuck!

I stretch my arm so far that it feels like it's going to pop out of my shoulder, but only two of my fingertips graze the handlebars.

My bike dives to the ground as my body flies forward. A feeling of dread and panic fills me as the hard ground comes up insanely fast.

"Fuck!" I scream into my helmet through a clenched jaw.

The ground is racing at me. I close my eyes.

And then...

Nothing.

CHAPTER TWO

THE BEST MEDICINE

Madison

"Dr. Madison Mendes," a tight voice echoes from down the hospital hall.

"Shit," I curse under my breath as I force out a tight smile and turn around. "Hello, Dr. Clark. I was just about to check in with you after my rounds."

"Your rounds can wait," he says, staring at me through his thick glasses. The bright lights on the ceiling are reflecting on his head under his thin comb-over. "Follow me."

He turns his tense body and storms down the hallway to his office. I feel an empty pit in my stomach as I follow him.

Two nurses, Carol and Shondra, give me matching smiles of sympathy as I pass their station. They saw the whole thing and know I'm about to get chewed out by my boss, the medical chief of staff.

I swallow hard as I step into his office where he's already

sitting behind his desk, staring at me with a stern look on his face. He looks pissed.

He's been looking at me that way for the past five days.

"Everything okay, Dr. Clark?" I ask with a wariness in my voice as I slide into the chair in front of him. I keep my back straight as he crosses his hairy arms over his chest—staring me down like an elementary school principal on a power trip.

"No," he snaps. "In your case, Dr. Mendes, everything is certifiably *not* okay."

He pulls out a file from the drawer and slaps it onto the desk between us.

I lean forward and read the name. *Patient Louis Newport.* He was in here last week. Ruptured spleen. Bleeding internally. I diagnosed him and got him onto the surgeon's table just in time.

"What's the problem?" I ask when he just stares at me with a smug look on his face.

"What is the problem?" he repeats with a laugh. "Look at the paperwork. It's a mess."

"The paperwork?" I say, staring at him in disbelief. "I saved the man's life."

"Saving lives is your job," he says, dismissing it with a wave of his hand. He picks up the stapled papers and waves them around in front of me. "*This* is also your job. And it's unsatisfactory at best. Sloppy handwriting, writing outside the lines, and you missed your initials here."

He tosses the papers back onto the desk and stares at me with a triumphant look on his weasely face.

"Is this about Anabelle?" I ask.

His hard look and authoritative demeanor crumbles like a house of cards. The threatening man who was sitting in front of me is gone—replaced with a wet-eyed, sniveling pathetic shell of a man.

"Did she mention me?" he asks, staring at me with wide hopeful eyes.

"Um," I say, trying to stall. He's wringing his hands as he starts breathing heavier, barely holding himself together.

He grabs his cellphone off the desk and looks at it with a hope in his eyes that quickly disappears once he sees that she didn't text him.

The text he's looking for is from my best friend Anabelle who dumped him after three dates. I'm so glad I set them up.

"I keep calling her," he says, looking frustrated as he runs his hand through his thin comb-over. "I always get her voicemail. Do you think she got the flowers I sent?"

I glance back at the door as my heart starts pounding. "I'm not sure," I say with a gulp. "Like I said, I haven't talked to her."

He frowns as he squeezes the cellphone in his hand, turning his knuckles white. "I better send her some more, just in case."

"No," I say when he hits a button that lights up his phone. "Maybe you should just give her some space."

Anabelle definitely received the flowers. All four dozen of them. She also received the oversized teddy bear that went straight into the dumpster, the chocolates that I helped her eat, and the singing Lady Gaga telegram who was no lady at all. Nothing says romance like a poorly dressed transvestite singing *Poker Face* in the hallway of your apartment building.

"I've given her space," he snaps. "What more does she want?"

A galaxy of space from what she's told me.

"Maybe," I stammer as I drop my eyes to the desk. "Maybe you two just aren't meant to be?"

His wet eyes narrow sharply on me, causing me to lean back involuntarily.

"That's the woman I want to marry," he says, taking heavy breaths like an angry bull. "We *will* get married. And *you* will help that become a reality."

I shift uncomfortably in my seat. "I will?"

"Yes," he says, picking up Mr. Newport's file off the desk. "Or we're going to have bigger problems than just sloppy handwriting."

"Sir," I say as my stomach hardens. "I think we should separate our work lives from our personal lives. I'm worried they're getting too muddled together."

He grins as he looks over the form. "And I think you should give Anabelle a call to put in a good word for me. Or you might not have a work life anymore to worry about."

My cheeks get hot as I stand up and shuffle to the door. I want to give him a piece of my mind for threatening my job over his dried-up sex life, but I just swallow it down instead. He's heartbroken and not acting rationally. Maybe in a few days he'll start thinking clearer.

I slip into a supply closet after leaving his office and sit on a stack of folded sheets as I dial Anabelle.

"Give me a second, sweetie," she says when she answers. *"I'm just ordering."*

I lean back against the wall and close my eyes as I listen to her ordering a late dinner at the drive-through.

"Yeah, I'll take the chicken burger with a salad... You know what? Fuck it. Give me the fries. Do you have turkey burgers instead of chicken?"

All I hear is a muffled sound from the drive-through speaker, but whatever they're saying, Anabelle doesn't like it.

"*Well, maybe people would order it if you had it on the freaking menu. Ever think of that?*"

More muffled sounds.

"*A bottled water... No, wait. I'll take a Coke. No. A chocolate milkshake. Large.*"

I hear more muffled sounds, and then she's back. "*Sorry about that, sweetie. I was just ordering a salad for dinner. Work has been c-ra-zy. How do people have time to cook anymore?*"

I'm about to call her on her 'salad' when I decide that it's better not to get on her bad side right before asking for a favor.

"I just had an interesting talk with Mitchell," I say instead.

"*Who?*"

"Dr. Mitchell Clark," I say with a roll of my eyes. "My boss who you dated."

"*Ew.*" I can hear the disgust in her voice through the phone. "*And we never dated.*"

"You went on *three* dates."

"*As a favor to you.*"

"I thought you'd like him."

She's laughing so hard that I have to pull the phone from my ear. "*That guy?!? Madison, he proposed to me on the third date! The third freaking date. I know I'm lovable, but come on!*"

"He's not *that* bad." He's definitely *that* bad.

"*You know what he has tattooed on his arm? Alf.*"

"Alf? Like the alien guy?"

"*Yes. Like the alien guy. He showed it to me proudly. God knows I could barely see it under all of his thick arm and shoulder hair.*"

"You wanted me to hook you up with a doctor and I did," I say, starting to panic.

"*Yeah, but I was thinking George Clooney in ER, and the guy you set me up with was more like Dr. Evil from Austin Powers. He had a comb-over! Why would you set me up with a guy who has a comb-over?"*

Looking back on it, I can see that it was a mistake, but at the time I just wanted my boss to have a distraction so that he would get off my back. Talk about a backfire. He's even worse now than he was before.

"Can you just call him back?" I plead. "He's making my life a living hell."

"I did my part, sweetie," she says. *"I'm out. Plus, I'm already seeing someone."*

"You are?" How does she find these guys so fast? Anabelle seems to have a date every weekend. I'm lucky if I have one a year. "Where do you find these guys?"

"It's not hard," she says. *"Just put down whatever boring medical textbook you're reading, unbutton the top three buttons of your shirt, walk out onto the sidewalk, stick your tits in the air, and wait. It's like fishing, really. Throw the bait out there and wait for the fish to nibble."*

"That's so romantic," I say with a roll of my eyes.

"It's more romantic than watching Netflix every night by yourself. Gotta go. My salad is ready."

"Enjoy your fries, I mean *salad*," I say with a grin before hanging up. I walk out of the closet and find my resident waiting at the door of my office.

"Here's some medicine for the doctor," Ralph says as he hands me a foam cup of coffee.

It's cold, weak, and tastes like someone used it as an ashtray—Cherry Valley Hospital's finest brew. But I still drink it. I wouldn't be able to get through my grueling twelve-hour shifts without it. Especially when those grueling shifts start at ten P.M. like the one tonight.

"Thanks, Ralph," I say between sips. "Let's get started. What do we have first?"

My resident-in-training pulls the clipboard out from under his arm and frowns as he looks it over. His long shaggy brown hair falls over his furrowed brow whenever he concentrates. I'd like to prescribe this kid a haircut.

I'm already moving down the hall as he struggles to keep up while still looking over the notes.

"Walter is still here," he says as he narrowly avoids the garbage can. "The day shifters still haven't diagnosed him. I suggest we take more blood and—"

"Who?" I ask, skidding to a stop.

"Walter," he says, furrowing his brow as he looks at me in confusion. "The accountant. The big guy with the bushy mustache."

"Oh," I say with a quick shake of my head before I start walking again. "You mean Mr. Thatcher."

"Sorry," he mutters when he catches up to me. "I thought you knew his first name."

"I don't want to know anything but the patient's last name and medical condition," I say as we pass the elevators.

"How come?" Ralph asks. "Wouldn't it be better if—"

"Look," I say, interrupting him as I spin around. "Never get close with a patient. Never get personal. Never get attached. When you're in this building, it should only be about medicine."

He brushes the long hair out of his eyes, and I get a strong urge to grab the nearest scalpel and do some surgery on his bangs.

"But maybe you could help the patients more if you open up a little," he says with the wide innocent eyes of a resident-in-training. He hasn't been through what I've been through. He doesn't know what I know. He doesn't know how hard this place can be.

He doesn't know the kind of devastation that can result from bringing your personal feelings onto the job. I know. And I'm *never* going to put myself in that kind of position again.

"Maybe if we get to know them we can use that information to help them better," Ralph continues, sounding so childlike, so naive. He reminds me of me when I started. "Love and compassion can heal too. Isn't love the best medicine?"

I step in close, locking my battle-hardened eyes on him. "*Medicine* is the best *medicine*."

My pudgy sidekick takes a defeated breath and drops his eyes to the floor.

I rest a hand on his shoulder. He's still young and thinks he knows it all, but after he loses a few, he'll be singing a different tune.

"Just keep any emotions inside here," I say tapping his chest, "until after your shift. Keep all that love for Lacey and the new pups."

He looks up at me and nods.

"How's that going?" I ask as we continue walking. The stray Labrador that Ralph's roommate brought home had been pregnant, and she recently gave birth. On his living room carpet.

"How do you think it's going?" he asks with a shake of his head. "I have nine puppies pissing, shitting, chewing, and drooling in my little apartment. Do you want one? They're really cute."

"Yeah," I say with a laugh. "They sound adorable. But I'll pass."

I step into Mr. Thatcher's room with Ralph on my heels.

He's lying in the hospital bed, gazing down at the picture frame in his hands. I try to keep my eyes off it, but I see that it's a young pretty girl. Probably his daughter.

The room smells like fresh flowers from the arrangement beside him, mixed with the sterilizing smell of bleach.

"Hello, Mr. Thatcher," I say as his heart monitor beeps steadily in the background.

"Good evening, Dr. Mendes," he says, placing the picture frame on the nightstand beside him. I keep my eyes off it. I don't want to know anything but his symptoms. His face breaks out into a wide smile when he sees Ralph behind me.

"Did you finish it?" Mr. Thatcher asks as Ralph walks past me and sits on his bed. "I've been dying to find out." My resident grabs the patient's hand in his and smiles.

Ralph shakes his head as I watch with confusion. "One chapter to go."

"Promise me you'll let me read it when you're done," Mr. Thatcher says.

"You'll be the first one I give it to. I promise. Hopefully, you'll be out of here by then and you can read it in your favorite chair."

Walter smiles. "As long as I'm out before my daughter's wedding, I'll be happy."

I force out a cough, and they both look up at me.

"I'm writing a Sci-Fi book," Ralph says with a nervous grin. "Walter helped me with some ideas for the end."

I resist the urge to shake my head as I grab the clipboard at the foot of the patient's bed.

"Still having abdominal pains, Mr. Thatcher?" I ask.

"Yes."

"Has the severity of them increased? Pain-wise?"

"No. They're just as bad as before."

I tap my pen on the clipboard as I look it over. This guy's

case is a hard one to crack. Abdominal pains. Kidney damage. High blood pressure.

"Dr. Preston," I say, nodding to Ralph. "Take some blood from Mr. Thatcher. I want to run some more tests."

Ralph smiles at the patient as he gets up. "Maybe I'll rename the villain after you," he says with a laugh.

"Nah," Mr. Thatcher says with a shake of his head. "I like Doctor Mendestra better."

I follow Ralph out into the hall, grabbing his arm as he hurries away. "Doctor Mendestra?" I ask him with my eyebrows raised.

He smiles nervously. "She's an evil alien from planet Turkot."

"It sounds suspiciously close to my name," I say, pulling him closer as I narrow my eyes on him. "Doctor Mendes?"

He cringes. "Coincidence?"

"Sounds like a Freudian slip to me," I say, squeezing my grip on him.

I let him go and take a deep breath. "Ralph," I say, softening my voice. "This is what I was talking about. You get too close to the patients. What if he dies tonight? Or tomorrow?"

"Or what if knowing that his doctor cares keeps him alive for an extra night?" Ralph turns and hurries away to get the syringe before I can respond.

A small part of me envies his wide-eyed optimism, but a larger part of me wants to call him an idiot. He should keep his feelings to himself and let the medicine do its job.

My thigh buzzes and I pull out my phone. It's a text from Anabelle with a picture of Alf. *In a few years, guys who look like this are going to be your only prospects. Get 'em while you're still hot!*

I roll my eyes as I slide my phone into my pocket, grab

my now stone-cold coffee, and continue down the hall to finish my rounds. But Anabelle's words keep lingering in my head. I do have to do something. I have to be proactive. I can't stand here thinking that Mr. Right is just going to bump into me.

"Ow," I shout as a stretcher slams into my ass, making me spill my cold coffee all over my shirt.

"Sorry," one of the ambulance drivers says as he rushes past me. There's a man lying on the stretcher groaning. Tim, the ambulance driver, looks back over his shoulder as he rushes down the hallway. "Coming, Dr. Mendes?"

"Yeah," I say with a sigh as I squeeze the excess coffee out of my shirt. "I'm just redesigning my outfit first."

"Well, make it quick," he says when he stops at the elevators. "We have a hot one here."

My mouth drops when I hurry over and take a closer look at him.

"You got that right," I mumble under my breath. He's definitely a hot one.

Gorgeous, in fact. Even with the black eye and dried blood on his face, he's gorgeous. His dark hair is matted with blood and dirt, but strangely it suits him.

My eyes wander down his shirtless body, looking for injuries, but all I can see is a massive chest, shredded abs, sculpted tattooed arms, and colorful motocross pants.

He's perfect. I have to save him. I have an obligation to the human race to save this guy. He's too beautiful to have his DNA eliminated from the species. He has to reproduce.

For the sake of all humanity.

"What happened to him?" I ask Tim as the elevator bings open and we push him inside.

"Dirt bike injury," he says as I press my stethoscope to

his hard chest. "He was competing in the Motocross Championship and wasn't wearing his seatbelt."

I stare at the patient's face as I listen to his heart. The rate is fast. Just like mine.

"We'll get you fixed up, Mr. Right," I whisper to him only loud enough for him to hear.

He opens his green eyes a crack, and looks up at me through the glossiness. His mouth curls up into a weak smile.

The moment is over too soon. The elevator door bings open, and we rush him out to the ER.

It's time to get to work.

CHAPTER THREE

THE BEST MEDICINE

Madison

I'm on hour six of my twelve-hour shift when one of the nurses named Shondra peeks her head into the examination room where I'm putting a cast on a drunken girl's broken arm. The girl was dancing on the bar in a club when she slipped on some spilled vodka and then did a spill of her own, right onto the floor, breaking her arm in the process.

It was a closed fracture, so she'll be fine, although she'll be waking up with more than a hangover tomorrow.

"I can finish that up for you," Shondra says as the girl snores on the examination table. "You're needed in room 312. Mr. Winters is awake."

"Who?" I ask as I stand up, letting Shondra take my place.

"Mr. Motorcycle," she says with a wicked grin. "He can rev my engine any day."

I turn away from her to hide my blushing cheeks. I've been thinking about him for the past five hours, obsessively wondering if he was going to wake up during my shift.

He was banged up pretty badly. He had some serious spinal cord compression, which is going to limit his mobility for a while, but he's really lucky he didn't break his back. I gave him an epidural steroid injection to relieve some of the swelling and the worst of the pain, but it's too early to tell if he's going to need surgery or not.

On top of that, he had a few gashes that needed stitches, a fractured rib, and a slight concussion.

But it's not his injuries that are on my mind. I can't stop thinking of how his hard, muscular body felt under my trembling fingertips.

Stay professional, Madison. Save it for Mr. Sparkles.

I take a deep breath and leave the room as a warm shiver flows through me. *I better stop and get some batteries for Mr. Sparkles on the way home. I think I'm going to need some backups.*

My heart is pounding nervously when I arrive at his room. One of the nurses, Takara, is in there with him. She's giggling like a teenage girl after her first kiss. *So unprofessional...*

I take a deep breath, fix my hair, and walk inside. Mr. Winters' eyes lock on me, and I involuntarily freeze on the spot.

His green eyes take me by surprise. They're as bright as a patch of grass in the desert, as striking as a jade gemstone atop a pile of dull rocks. Green has never been so sexy. Did you know that green could be sexy?

His sexy lips curl up into a smile, and it awakens something dormant inside of me—something that wants to kick

Takara out of the room and do things that will get my medical license revoked. He's lying on the reclined bed with his naked chest and shredded abs in full glorious view. His two tattooed arms are raised in slings to prevent his back from moving while the swelling in his spine goes down. Somehow, he's impossibly managing to make slings look sexy.

I don't know who helped him out of his gown and bunched it up around his waist, but they're about to get a raise—even if it has to come out of my own paycheck.

"I'll be back in a bit, Shane," Takara says as she leaves with a wide grin on her face. I don't know why, but I have a sudden urge to hit her over the head with my clipboard to put her in the coma ward.

It's just the two of us in the room now. I haven't been this nervous around a patient since my first day.

I can't seem to make my feet work, so I look down at the clipboard in my hands, seeing nothing but blurred words and cartoon hearts floating around me. I narrow my eyes, pretending like I'm reading, but all I'm doing is threatening the blood rushing to my cheeks to try and convince it to head the other way.

Stop turning my cheeks red or I'll head straight to the blood donor clinic where they'll put you in a bag and freeze you. Would you like that, blood?

Shockingly, my blood doesn't listen.

Plan B. Time for a pep talk.

All right, Madison. You're a professional. Start acting like it. This man is hurt and needs a qualified doctor, not a blushing schoolgirl who wants to run her hands all over those big arms and sexy chest and... I wonder what those abs feel like... God, that chest is pure perfection. I wonder if that bitch Takara gets to give him a sponge bath. Would it be against the rules for a doctor to give a patient a sponge bath? I'll check the manual once I finish my—

"Hello?" he says, waving his hand at me, ripping me out of my perverted trance.

"Yes," I say with a cough. "Hello. I'm Dr. Mendes. I'm going to be your doctor."

"Lucky me," he answers with a grin.

"No," I say as I narrow my eyes on him. "Not lucky you. You're in bad shape with some serious injuries. You almost died."

He shrugs his round shoulders. "It's not the first time."

"Well, it was almost the last."

He just smiles. His complete lack of giving any shits that he almost died gets to me. *Why is he not terrified right now?*

"Are you single?" he asks.

Now he's really getting to me.

"You can't feel your legs, and the first question you ask your doctor is if she's single?"

"I want to get the important stuff out of the way first," he says with a grin.

I just glare at him as my chest tightens.

"The nurse told me it was only temporary," he says when it's clear that I'm not going to answer.

"The nurse told you," I repeat under my breath. The annoyance is clear in my voice. "Was *she* single?"

"I don't know," he says with a sexy smile. "She's not my type."

I let out an audible gulp. *I'm his type?*

"So, is that a yes or a no?" he asks. He glances at my ring-less wedding ring finger and smiles.

I can't believe the nerve of this guy. He has temporary paralysis, a fractured rib, a mild concussion, his arms are in slings, and the only information he's asking is about my personal life.

"You must have hit your head harder than I thought," I say as I approach his bed.

"No," he says with a laugh. "I'm always like this."

"Well," I say as I sit on the side of his bed with a straight face. "Good to know that your concussion didn't hamper your ability to sexually harass women."

He flashes his beautiful white teeth. "We finally agree on something."

"Mr. Winters..."

"Shane," he says, interrupting me.

"*Mr. Winters*," I repeat with a little more force in my voice. "You almost broke your back. This is serious. We took an MRI of your spine, and the nerves around your vertebrae showed some significant swelling. We gave you a steroid injection while you were asleep, and you'll be on anti-inflammatory medication until the swelling goes down. You're going to be immobile for a while."

"How long is a while?"

"A few days," I say. "It depends. You'll gradually start getting the sensation back in your legs, but until then you won't be able to walk."

"So, I'll be your guest for a few days?"

"You'll be my *patient*," I correct.

"What about these?" he asks, looking at the slings wrapped around his arms.

"Those will be off in a few hours," I say. "We want to keep your back stabilized while the steroids do their job. Do you have any more questions?"

"When you go home," he says, staring at me with his mischievous green eyes, "is there going to be a man in your—"

"Questions about your condition," I say, interrupting him. I roll my eyes. "Forget it. Mr. Winters, I have to examine you now."

"All right," he says with a grin. "Finally getting to the good part."

Is this guy for real?

I want to be mad at him, but I'm too shocked by his boldness. And a part of me kind of likes it.

I've been avoiding looking at him too closely, but now I don't have a choice. My breath starts to quicken as I place my stethoscope in my ears and lean in close to him. His intense green eyes are locked on mine.

His right eye is black from the accident, but the darkness on the skin around it just makes the striking green color pop even more. It's the first time I'm looking at his face up close, and it's making me light-headed. His nose is a tad crooked like it was broken in an accident long ago but never fixed. It should ruin his look, but instead, it just makes him look that much sexier. A flaw that adds to the perfection.

"I'm going to check your heart rate," I say as I look down at his massive tattooed chest. I swallow hard as I press the tip of my stethoscope to his left pec and listen.

His heart is racing. "Your heart rate is up."

He grins as he watches me. "It wasn't like this a minute ago."

Yeah. Mine wasn't either.

Our eyes meet again, and my heart pounds harder than ever.

You could cut the sexual chemistry with a scalpel.

"You have a beautiful look," he says with a voice that feels like soft leather. "What are you?"

"I'm a doctor," I answer curtly.

He laughs, and for some reason I feel like pulling out a notebook and writing poetry.

"I can see that," he says. "I can also see a hint of what? Puerto Rican?"

I let out a frustrated sigh. "Portuguese."

"Mom or dad?"

This is going too far. I've already violated my hard-fast rule of keeping personal stuff out of the examining room.

"Can we just focus on the examination?" I ask, getting flustered.

"You focus on your examination. I'll focus on mine."

I yank the stethoscope back down on my neck and glare at him. "This is inappropriate."

"Your eye twitches when you're upset," he says with an amused smile.

My jaw is clenched, my body tense. "I'm not upset."

"Look," he says with a grin. "It's twitching even more."

I get off the bed and stand up, staring down at him with heated eyes. "Would you like me to get a sedative to knock you out while I finish this?"

"No," he says with a shake of his head. "I want to be awake and alert when your hands are all over me."

"This is your last chance," I say as every nerve ending in my tense body tingles. "I'm going to examine your lower half now."

"Does my cock work?"

My head whips around and my eyes lock onto his.

He shrugs as he motions to the slings that his arms are strapped into. "I can't reach it. I can't tell if it works or not."

Finally, something he's worried about.

"It may not work for a couple of days," I say. "Or never."

I don't know why I lie to him, but I do. I guess I want to get him as flustered as he's gotten me.

But I may have gone overboard because he freaks the fuck out.

"Never?!?" he shouts, staring at me in panic. "Examine it. Please!"

I shake my head, not knowing what to do. I might have gone too far this time.

"I'm not going to touch it," I say with a hard swallow.

"Why not?" he asks, struggling to reach it. He's going to rip his arm out of the sling and do more damage to his back. "Just smack it around a bit."

"Stop moving," I say as I tighten his arm slings. "I'm not touching you there. It's highly inappropriate."

"It's a doctor's examination to see if it works," he says, staring at me with pleading eyes. "It's not sexual unless you put those pretty little lips on it."

My cheeks turn insanely hot.

"I'm sorry," he says after taking a deep breath. "That was inappropriate. But please. I need my cock. The women of the world need my cock."

There's a tenseness in my stomach as I watch him with uncertainty. He is my patient, and he's making a medical request. I shouldn't deny him a medical examination just because the thought of his big long package is getting me warm between the legs.

"Please," he begs.

"Fine," I say as I roll up my sleeves.

I talk to myself as I reach down and grab his gown that's bunched up around his waist. *This is a medical exam. You're a professional, and this is all part of your job. You're definitely not going to relive this moment tonight when you pull out Mr. Sparkles from your nightstand drawer.*

I nearly gasp when I pull down the thin fabric and see his long thick cock trailing down his muscular legs.

Wow. He's a lot bigger than Mr. Sparkles.

I'm breathless to the point where I'm almost panting as I stare at it. It's beautiful. I'm tempted to take pictures for his file. A file that I would definitely work on at home, probably at the same time as I work on myself.

Arousal begins coursing through my tingling body, settling between my legs.

"I'm going to begin the examination," I say in a voice that's much lower than normal.

He cranes his neck up, watching as I poke the shaft with my finger. It moves, and I flinch—jumping back in shock.

"What is it?" he asks. He still looks terrified that his cock won't work again.

I can't blame him. If I had a cock as beautiful as that, I would be terrified too.

"Nothing," I say, taking a deep breath as I try to compose myself. I have an idea. It's not a good idea, but it's all I got.

I pull a pencil from my front pocket and poke his dick with the eraser. "Do you feel that?"

"Are you kidding me?" he asks, staring at me in shock. "Just grab it."

I hold in a breath as I reach down and take it in my trembling hand. It's so big, and all I can think about is finishing the examination with my mouth.

"Do you feel this?" It's only four words, but two of them crack. I feel like there's a frog in my throat.

"No," he says with a shake of his head.

He may not feel it, but it definitely still works. His shaft hardens in my hand as he starts to get an erection.

I jerk my hand back like I just touched a hot stove and yank his gown back down to cover it. I'll be thinking about his dick enough. I don't need to see it fully hard. That will make me become an obsessive crazy woman.

"I'll be right back," I say, racing to the door.

"Where are you going?" he asks as I yank the door open, and hurry into the hall. I close the door and lean against it as my heart pounds.

I quickly slip the stethoscope into my ears and check my own heart, worried that it's going to explode. It's thumping like a rabbit on speed, but so far, no explosions.

Is that what you call professional? I chastise myself as I hurry down the hall, looking for Ralph.

I grab the resident I'm training and drag him back to the room to finish the examination for me.

Shane frowns when he sees that I've brought a third wheel to the party.

"This is Dr. Preston," I say, presenting Ralph. "He's going to finish the examination. I have to take care of another emergency."

Changing my wet panties constitutes an emergency, right?

Shane starts to protest as I head to the door. "Wait!" he says as Ralph steps forward and yanks down his gown. "God, your knuckles are so hairy!"

I hurry into the hall, unsuccessfully trying to settle some of the overpowering arousal taking over my body.

Yup. Definitely going to need fresh batteries for Mr. Sparkles.

Available at www.AuthorKimberlyFox.com

ALSO BY KIMBERLY FOX

The Best Medicine

Heavy Turbulence

Well Hung Over in Vegas

Bad Boys on the Beach Series:

Cancun

Belize

Aruba

Box Set of All Three

The Hitman's Baby

The Hitman's Second Chance